"Don't tell me you think that I'm so desperate for a woman that I'd go to bed with a computer?" Dylan demanded increduously

"A very attractive computer," Julianna pointed out. "I'm told that terran men find the voluptuous physiques of the sex androids irresistible."

"Her design was appealing," he admitted. "But I've always been extremely choosy about my female companions."

She arched a disbelieving brow. "My field studies have confirmed that the average terran male is far from discriminating."

Dylan had a sudden urge to yank her into his arms and kiss that haughty, superior Sarnian expression right off her face. "When you get to know me better, Juls, you'll discover that I'm definitely not your average terran male."

His eyes swept her from head to toe. "As to female physical attributes, I'm flexible—sex is ninety percent mental."

"To Sarnians sexual congress is always mental," Julianna gasped.

He gave her another of those warm, intimate, horrendously dangerous smiles. "I said ninety percent. If you make the mistake of skipping that important ten percent, you're missing one helluva lot."

Dear Reader,

"Second to the right and then straight on till morning."
Peter Pan's words capture the human spirit at its most
adventurous—the desire to find out what's around the
next corner. JoAnn Ross has taken this same
determination and crafted two wonderful love stories
that we just had to make Editor's Choice novels. Each
stands alone as a fulfilling romance. *Star-Crossed
Lovers* and *Moonstruck Lovers* are about people falling
in love—only *Moonstruck Lovers* takes us on a
rollicking space adventure.

This is what Temptation does best—breaking a few
barriers to give you the most contemporary, sensual
romances possible. Nineteen-ninety-three continues to
be an exciting year with our Lovers & Legends
miniseries, and more Editor's Choice novels, including
a sizzling sexy story by Mallory Rush in June called
Love Slave—need we say more? Glenda Sanders's ghost
trilogy concludes with *Lovers Secrets,* available this
summer.

And yes, "Second to the right, and then straight till
morning," were also Captain Kirk's last words in Star
Trek VI.

Here's to adventure!

Birgit Davis-Todd
Senior Editor

P.S. JoAnn would love to hear from her readers.
Write to her:
       JoAnn Ross
       c/o Harlequin Temptation
       225 Duncan Mill Road
       Don Mills, Ontario
       M3B 3K9

MOONSTRUCK LOVERS

JoAnn Ross

Harlequin Books

TORONTO • NEW YORK • LONDON
AMSTERDAM • PARIS • SYDNEY • HAMBURG
STOCKHOLM • ATHENS • TOKYO • MILAN
MADRID • WARSAW • BUDAPEST • AUCKLAND

To my editors, Birgit Davis-Todd, who, for the
past eight years has always encouraged me to take
risks, and Malle Vallik, whose constant good
humor and shared love of adventure makes
writing these stories so much fun.

Published March 1993

ISBN 0-373-25536-5

MOONSTRUCK LOVERS

1

APPEARANCES WERE definitely deceiving.

Dylan Prescott's top-secret laboratory, hidden away deep in the woods on the remote island of Castle Mountain, Maine, and known locally as "the brain factory," did not look like a mad scientist's lair.

There were no steaming, bubbling sulfurous beakers, no petri dishes growing strange green alien lifeforms, no bodies of people trapped between the living and the dead, laid out on slabs with electrodes attached to their shaved heads.

The walls were not carved from thick gray stone taken from some medieval Transylvanian castle, but were constructed from an ordinary grade of Sheetrock purchased at a lumberyard in Bangor. Not a speck of damp, smelly mold darkened the glacier-white enamel paint, and no rats scurried furtively across the shiny tile floor to hide in dark corners.

There were no dark corners. The laboratory, brightly lit from the glowing bank of fluorescent lights overhead, resembled a hospital operating room; open-heart surgery could have been performed on any of the shiny stainless steel countertops.

Black steel filing cabinets lined the wall; atop an ebony desk a computer obediently hummed, numbers flashing across its screen in fluorescent orange print.

Two men worked in the laboratory on this cold February afternoon. If the energy radiating from Dylan Prescott and Bram Starbuck could have been harnessed, it would undoubtedly have been capable of heating the homes of every inhabitant of the island of Castle Mountain well into the next century. And beyond.

Starbuck was seated at the computer, a frown of concentration darkening his brow as his fingers moved deftly over the keyboard, turning complex mathematical algorithms into scientific visualization.

Outside the laboratory, a gentle snow fell. Inside, Starbuck and Dylan watched the monitor as the computer scanned its way through and around and past billions of miles and thousands of light-years.

Visuals of the universe burst forth in a dazzling display of furious fireworks: stars flaring, dying in cold black voids while worlds were being reborn from exploded remnants, whirling galaxies hurling heated gases in all directions, glittering stardust, blinding fireballs and speeding, spinning, flaming quasars.

Planets were scattered about like comet-tail dust over thousands of light-years; matter and light disappeared, sucked up by devouring black holes, disappearing from the screen, never to be seen again.

"It's the Milky Way," Dylan said unnecessarily as the glowing, spiraling band of starlight appeared on the screen.

Starbuck remembered all too clearly the thrill he'd received when he'd first seen those spiral arms extending outward from the mass of bight, scattering stardust.

"It won't be long now," he said. "You'd better get ready."

A shared feeling of expectation made the air crackle around them.

Dylan's heart picked up its beat as he stepped into the imaging circle he and Starbuck had constructed.

If everything went as planned, Dylan Prescott would go down in history as the man who proved time travel was possible. And more than that, by intricately charting the folds and warps of space, he intended to actually cut across not only light-years, but entire galaxies.

He would, Dylan knew, be famous. If he succeeded. But it was not the fame that had him risking his life this way. Nor was it a need for adventure, although that was an appealing aspect of his experiment. Most importantly, what he was about to do was quite simply, the fulfillment of a lifelong dream.

Long ago, one Halloween night, his mother had read aloud from a book entitled *The Sketch Book of Geoffrey Crayon, Gent.* Dylan had received the ancient, dusty, leather-bound book one week before, from his Grandmother Prescott, for his fifth birthday.

It was, his father had proudly told him, a first edition, signed by the author himself—Washington Irving. His father had gone on to tell him that the book had been in the Prescott family for six generations. But at the time, Dylan had been unimpressed by either the book's history or its value. Nor had he wondered why his grandmother would have chosen to bestow such a gift on a child.

Indeed, on that dark and stormy night, sneezing from the dust drifting off the book's yellowed pages, Dylan Prescott had felt betrayed. He had, after all, asked Gramma Prescott for the inorganic chemistry set—complete with periodic table chart—he'd seen listed in a *Young Explorers* catalogue. Instead, all he'd gotten was this crummy old book.

What was especially galling was that Charity, his twin sister, had received her request—a brand-new wedding Barbie doll, complete with two-story house and trousseau fit for a fairy-tale princess.

But when his mother got to the story of Rip Van Winkle, Dylan's irritation immediately disintegrated, like frosty morning mist over the harbor. Because from the time old Rip woke up from his nap, Dylan Prescott, youthful genius and scientific prodigy, was hooked on the idea of traveling through time.

Two years later, when he discovered H. G. Wells's *The Time Machine* in the library, he vowed to create a similar machine of his own.

Which now, with Bram Starbuck's valuable assistance, he had.

Dylan tightened his fingers around the compact quantum accelerator Starbuck had spent years developing. Starbuck's theory had been predicated on the idea that physics, not technology, held the ultimate answer to space travel.

Despite opposition from his own scientific community, Starbuck had believed that a person, aided by a pocket-size antimatter accelerator device, could travel through the galaxies in an astral, or ethereal body; that the component atoms that made up a person could be taken apart, transported through space utilizing the theory of quantum electrodynamics, then be put back together when they'd reached their destination.

Against all odds, and as improbable as it had sounded when Dylan had first learned of his friend's experiment, the molecular accelerator had successfully brought the Sarnian astrophysicist through dozens of galaxies to earth.

What had been even more amazing was his assertion that he'd gotten the idea from a textbook Dylan had not yet written. A book Starbuck had claimed was required reading at the Sarnian Science Institute. Two hundred years in the future.

Now Dylan hoped the accelerator would enable him to make that same journey in the opposite direction.

The accelerator was small enough to be held in a man's palm. More important, it included a miniature ecumenical translator that Starbuck assured Dylan would allow him to speak with the inhabitants of the faraway planet. The voice module for the translator was implanted in his middle ear.

A sparkling blue diamond, contributed by his sister, served as an electrical conductor. She'd willingly donated her engagement ring to the scientific project when she'd learned that having lost his powers of telekinesis on Earth, Starbuck was in need of a carbon-based crystallized stone to supply additional boost to the accelerator.

When Charity had given Starbuck the ring—the only thing she'd salvaged from her disastrous marriage—she'd believed that he and Dylan were planning to use it to send Starbuck back home. Dylan smiled, thinking of Charity's reaction when she learned that it was her twin brother who'd taken the interstellar trip instead.

Images flashed before Dylan's eyes with a blinding, strobelike effect.

"If I don't make it back in time, I want you and Charity to go ahead and get married without me," he shouted as he was pulled faster and faster toward the light.

In the beginning, he'd been against the romance between the time-traveling intergalactic traveler and his sister. But love had proven stronger than logic, and although Starbuck had valiantly tried to resist Charity's very feminine charms, ultimately, he'd failed.

In the end, Starbuck had chosen to stay on Earth with the woman he loved, which was why Dylan was on his way to Sarnia in his friend's place.

Lights—red, green, yellow and blue—flashed behind Dylan's closed lids. The light was a medley of wavelengths, surrounding him, radiating in all directions. His body felt as if it were being stung by a hundred, a thousand, angry yellow jackets.

"I want you both to be happy," Dylan managed to say on a harsh gasp.

"Don't worry." Starbuck watched Dylan flinch, and remembered vividly how painful his own transition had proven. "You're going to make it back in plenty of time to give the bride away."

The plan had, after all, been carefully thought out. They had also adjusted for the time warp caused by solar flares that had made Starbuck land on Earth two centuries earlier than he'd expected.

Fortunately, Sarnia possessed an atmosphere and gravitational pull remarkably similar to that of Earth, making it possible for Dylan Prescott to survive comfortably.

Dylan would land on the distant, domed planet two hundred years in the future, spend two weeks with Starbuck's sister, Julianna, lecturing to those same Sarnian scientists who'd refused to believe that Starbuck's theory of molecular astro-projection as a means of intergalactic space travel could ever work.

Then, after vindicating his friend's reputation and assuring both Julianna and Rachel Valderian, Starbuck's mother, that Starbuck was alive and well and happy, with Julianna's expert assistance, Dylan would return home.

Dylan felt a pulsing deep inside his body, the increasingly strong beats synchronizing with the flashing lights that were now the entire spectrum of the rainbow.

He was breaking apart. Disintegrating. Dissolving in the sparkling golden light.

"Tell my sister and my mother that I love them. And take care of Charity."

It was the last thing Dylan Prescott would say before vanishing from his laboratory.

And his planet.

The planet Sarnia
Moon date: Gamma 19.5

"THE PRISONER WILL STAND."

Julianna Valderian's expression was serene as she rose before the black-robed magistrate. A lifetime of practice kept her from revealing the anxiety bubbling away inside her.

The fact that the jury of nine male Sarnian Elders had taken only a brief recess before returning to the courtroom was not encouraging. Neither was the condemnation she could read in their cold, judgmental eyes.

"Has the jury reached a verdict?" the judge asked.

The jury foreman, a tall, distinguished gentleman in his late eighties, with a shock of silver hair, rose. Erothenes Lycurgus was a professor emeritus at the Sarnian Science Institute, where, until her arrest, Julianna had taught xenoanthropology.

At one time, her former department head had served as her much-respected mentor. Overlooking her gender, which in the strictly masculine confines of the university system should have restricted her prospects, Lycurgus had encouraged her to excel.

And now, although the elderly scholar was too properly restrained to reveal any emotion, as his glance briefly swept over her rigidly composed features, Julianna could sense his profound disappointment in his former honor student.

"We have, Your Honor."

"On the first count, what say you?"

Lycurgus's eyes met Julianna's. In them she could read resignation. And worse, yet, pity. "We, the legally impaneled jury of Elders, find the accused, Julianna Valderian, guilty of heresy."

Behind her, Julianna heard her mother, Rachel Valderian, gasp. And although she'd known all along that this verdict was coming, Julianna's hands, clasped together in front of her, turned to ice.

"And on the second count," the stone-faced Sarnian judge asked. "What say you?"

Julianna didn't so much as blink. But her fingernails were digging deep gouges into the tender flesh of her palms.

Lycurgus took a deep breath. For a fleeting moment his mask slipped, allowing Julianna to see that he was obviously pained by his colleagues' decision. This time he could not meet her steady, unblinking gaze.

"On the second count, we find the accused, Julianna Valderian, guilty of high treason."

Rachel's ragged, painful wail ripped through the room. Julianna's tawny eyes stung, not with tears for herself—after all, she'd known from the beginning the risk she was taking—but for her mother.

Rachel Valderian had recently lost her husband. Then her son, determined to prove his farfetched scientific theory, had disappeared without a trace. And now she was about to lose her daughter as well. No woman deserved such pain. Especially not one as warm and loving as Rachel.

"And is this verdict unanimous?" the judge asked the jury foreman.

Her former mentor squared his shoulders. His eyes met Julianna's again, but this time the compassion was gone. Instead, his gaze was as blank and unfeeling as that belonging to Julianna's house-droid.

"Yes. So say us all."

The judge turned to Julianna. "Julianna Valderian." He frowned darkly when he was forced to raise his voice to be heard over Rachel's wrenching sobs. "You have been found guilty of heresy and high treason. Do you have anything you wish to say before sentencing?"

Actually, Julianna could think of quite a few pithy comments, none of them the least bit complimentary. Neither would any of them serve to reverse the jury's decision. Besides, venting the frustration, anger and sense of betrayal she felt would only give her accusers the pleasure of saying that such display of emotional-ism was proof that women, especially those tainted with human blood, were intellectually inferior.

"No, Your Honor," she said with a calm that she was a very long way from feeling. Only the defiant tilt of her chin displayed her disdain with these proceedings. "I have nothing to say."

"Then it is the decision of this court that you will be banished to the moon Australiana." This too was not unexpected. "Where you shall remain in exile," the judge continued in that same deep monotone, "for the remainder of your life."

He turned toward the man standing in the corner of the room. "Bailiff, return the prisoner to her home, where she will remain under house arrest until trans-port can be arranged to the penal colony on Austra-liana."

His duty done, the black-robed magistrate pounded his gavel. "This Supreme Court of Sarnia is hereby ad-journed."

He rose and left the room, followed by the entirely male jury. The bailiff, clad in the black uniform and high boots of the Janurian Guard, approached. When Rachel Valderian rushed forward, intent on embracing her daughter, two additional guards grabbed her by the arms and began dragging her toward the high double doors at the back of the courtroom.

"Let her go." Julianna's voice was as steady and clear as a bell. Shaking the bailiff's hand off her shoulder, she made her way toward her mother. The courtroom spectators, unaccustomed to rebellion, obediently parted, allowing her to pass.

Her mother's unchecked tears caused Julianna far more pain than the judge's harsh sentence. "Don't worry." She put her arms around Rachel's slender shoulders and pressed her cheek against her mother's wet one. "Bram will be back soon," she promised, wishing she could believe that her brother would return safely to Sarnia. "You won't be alone."

"I'm not concerned for myself." Rachel drew in a ragged breath, struggling for calm. "It's you I'm worried about. To think of you ... in that place ..." Her warm amber eyes, so like her daughter's, brimmed over again.

"I'll be fine."

It was a lie, and both mother and daughter knew it. The truth was, the government could not risk Julianna's heretical views becoming widely known. Even to the exiled population on Australiana.

Although capital punishment had been technically illegal on Sarnia for more than six centuries, fatal accidents occurring during transport to the penal colony were not entirely unknown. The chances of Julianna reaching the lunar outpost were slim to none.

"The Valderian name is not without influence," Rachel reminded her. Her slumped shoulders, beneath the silver gown that signified her as a member of the ruling class, squared. A flash of renewed determination shone in her eyes. "You are descended from the Ancient Ones, Julianna. Your attorney should have pointed that out more often during your defense."

"I don't think that would have helped, Mother."

Julianna didn't want to hurt her mother further by pointing out that in this highly stratified society, her father had already irrevocably tarnished the Valderian name by his marriage to a terran—Julianna's mother.

All her life, her parentage had been held against Julianna. Despite the fact that she was half human, until this recent debacle, she'd always behaved like a true Sarnian, steadfastly eschewing the emotional in favor of logic.

But, although she'd always done her best to adhere to the Sarnian way of logic and truth, not once, in all her twenty-five years, had she ever considered denying her humanness. Nor had her brother.

To do so would have been to deny their mother, and since Sarnian children were brought up to respect and revere their elders, such behavior would have been highly illogical and totally without reason.

Besides, both Julianna and Starbuck had known intuitively that such denial would have pained them in some intrinsic way they could not quite understand.

Rachel appeared not to have heard Julianna's soft demurral. "And you're right about your brother returning," she said with an encouragingly maternal smile that only wobbled slightly. "When he does, he will do whatever it takes to get you released. In the meantime, I will find another barrister to appeal your conviction."

Julianna tried to return her mother's smile and failed. Miserably. When she went to embrace Rachel again, a large cruel hand curled around her shoulder and roughly jerked her away.

"Time to go," the bailiff muttered in a guttural Janurian accent. When he snapped the tight metal bands around Julianna's wrists, her mother began to weep again.

Julianna knew, that for whatever time she managed to stay alive, she would never forget the anguish on her mother's still lovely face.

An hour after the jury's verdict, Erothenes Lycurgus arrived at Julianna's home. Utilizing his unquestioned authority as one of the Sarnian ruling class, he dismissed her armed guards, professing his need to speak to the prisoner alone.

"I tried to warn you," he told Julianna. His expression was grim, displaying emotions he'd spent more than eighty-seven years successfully suppressing.

Julianna sighed. "I know."

"It was bad enough when you insisted on constantly speaking out on women's equality. But when you called the Ancient Ones hypocrites—"

"Aren't they?" Julianna interrupted hotly. "How could they preach peace and reason after the atrocities they committed?"

"That is a blatant untruth!" When the elderly man glanced around nervously, as if searching for spies, Julianna belatedly realized that eavesdropping devices had been installed inside her home.

"It is the truth," Julianna corrected calmly. What more could the Ruling Council do to her? "I have proof that a vibrant, matriarchal society existed on Sarnia long before the arrival of our ancestors."

"There can be no proof of such a preposterous charge."

"You are wrong. I have documentation that women ruled Sarnia in peace and prosperity for several centuries with a vision of equality for all."

Julianna frowned darkly as she considered the truth she'd uncovered in her crusade for female rights on the male-dominated planet. "At least there was peace until the Ancient Ones arrived on Sarnia at the bequest of Elder Mother's husband, who lusted for wealth. And power."

"Need I remind you that the Ancient Ones were your own ancestors?" Her former mentor's tone was a bit too sharp for a proper Sarnian, Julianna considered.

"They were murderers," she countered, "committing a bloody purge to gain absolute control."

"There is no evidence of that," he repeated doggedly.

"Oh, yes, there is."

"Then prove your claim," he suggested. A sly look crept into his eyes. "Show us this alleged verification."

Julianna realized that his mission in coming here today was to convince her to hand over her evidence to the Ruling Council. She also knew, without the slightest doubt, that the Elders would immediately destroy it.

"Someday the truth will be known," she insisted quietly. Meanwhile, until that time, the diary and letters that proved the veracity of her claim would remain carefully hidden.

He shook his head sadly. "Despite your venerated family name, I always feared your terran blood would eventually win out. Your father would be very disappointed in you. You have brought dishonor to the esteemed Valderian name."

Julianna lifted her chin. "My father," she said slowly, deliberately, "taught my brother and me to always tell the truth. That being the case, my father would be proud."

A frustrated red flush rose from the collar of his silver tunic. "I came here tonight, in the name of charity, to offer you one last opportunity to put this foolishness behind you.

"Proclaim your guilty lie, Julianna Valderian. Tell the court that you swore falsely. Allow the physicians to treat your disruptive mental condition.

"And then," he said, holding out a very juicy carrot, "your sentence will be commuted and you can take your place once again in Sarnian society."

"To say that I swore falsely would be a lie," Julianna said with quiet dignity, and not a little stubbornness. "As a properly reared Sarnian, I do not lie."

"No properly reared Sarnian would behave as you have behaved," he countered. "You shall be banished, Julianna. For all of your days. And your traitorous underground women's movement will have been quashed."

"Perhaps," she agreed. "Perhaps not."

His white brows crashed down toward his aristocratic nose. "What do you mean?"

"I mean, there is always a chance I will return to Sarnia to tell my truth."

"No one has ever escaped from Australiana."

"Perhaps I'll be the first," Julianna responded daringly. "And if not, believe me, Erothenes Lycurgus, the council may be able to silence me. But the women's movement will live long after my ashes have become space dust."

His answering frown was dark and final. "May the ancient gods have mercy on your pitiful soul," the old man said.

And then he was gone.

Later that night she lay on her back on her sleeping pallet, staring bleakly out the window at the glowing red ball that was the faraway moon, Australiana.

Although, unlike her brother, she was completely mindblind, lacking in Sarnian telepathy, Julianna imagined she could still hear her mother's anguished sobs.

Pulling the pillow over her head, Julianna curled up in a tight ball, closed her eyes and wished for the long, lonely night to end.

2

IT WAS LATE AFTERNOON. The moon, preparing to rise, hovered just below the western horizon, casting a muted, rosy glow over the landscape. At the same time, the vast yellow orb of the Sarnian sun was setting in the east, splitting that soft pink light with dazzling fingers of gold.

The inhabitants of the domed planet were busy preparing for Truthfest, the annual observation of the arrival of the Ancient Ones. The two-week-long celebration was the one time in the year when even the most rational Sarnians, aided by vast amounts of Enos Dew, tended to loosen the reins on their emotions.

Commuters, racing home from their government offices, were smiling in anticipation. Their thoughts focused on the festivities of the upcoming days, they failed to notice the sparkling bits of matter reassembling themselves outside the quartzalite windows of their speeding air shuttles. "It works!"

Dylan stared around him in wonder. He flexed his long fingers, fascinated by the way they were materializing before his very eyes. As he watched, the rest of his body quickly followed.

"Hot damn," he shouted, "it actually works!" He could feel the grin practically splitting his face in half.

A grin that faded when he realized that he was standing face-to-face with a pair of very large, very ugly men clad in black uniforms. A thick, leathery frontal ridge ran along the men's foreheads; a primitive violence lurked in their eyes.

"You're late," one of the men accused in a guttural language. The calm female voice of Starbuck's ecumenical translator explained the language to be Janurian, then obligingly decoded.

"I got held up."

Starbuck had assured Dylan that since English was the chosen language of those terrans living on Sarnia, he would be able to make himself understood. Any differences in syntax would merely be considered due to him being from off-planet.

The men exchanged a look. "Truthfest is about to begin. We get paid overtime for holidays."

"Well, I'm here now," Dylan pointed out.

With a shrug of his massive shoulders, the larger of the two men punched a code into what resembled a solar pocket calculator. His fingers were thick as sausages; rough black hair covered the knuckles. He was, Dylan considered, horrendously ugly. He was also not a man Dylan would want to meet in a dark alley.

The metal door panel behind him slid silently open.

"Your prisoner awaits."

"Prisoner?"

Deciding that somehow he and Starbuck must have miscalculated, causing him to land somewhere other than Julianna Valderian's home, Dylan entered the gleaming white building.

The door slid closed behind him, leaving him all alone in the foyer. The furniture, what little there was of it, was low, sleek and coolly modern. It also looked highly uncomfortable.

He found himself comparing it with the cozy, somewhat shabby home he sometimes shared with Charity on Castle Mountain, the home that had belonged to his Grandmother Prescott, and felt a tinge of homesickness, which he promptly quashed.

He would make it home, Dylan vowed. After completing his mission here on Sarnia, after vindicating Starbuck's theory, he would return to Earth in time to watch his sister marry the man who, in the beginning, he'd admittedly viewed as a fascinating experiment. A man who had become, in only a few short weeks, his best friend.

A man whose face seemed to be looking at him from atop a sleek black pillar. Intrigued, Dylan was studying the three-dimensional hologram when two more men, twins to the pair outside the door, and dressed in identical uniforms and knee-high black boots, entered the room.

Between them was a woman who could only be Julianna Valderian.

Starbuck had told Dylan that his sister was intelligent. And frustratingly stubborn. But now, as his appreciative gaze swept over her, Dylan wondered why his friend had neglected to mention her beauty.

She was dressed in a silvery blue gown created of some fiber so soft and silky it reminded him of the angel hair his mother had put on the Christmas tree one year. The neck of the floor-length gown was high, the sleeves flowing to her unpainted fingertips. Her body was reed slender, but from the way the material clung to her figure, Dylan could see that she had curves in all the right places.

Her hair was a gleaming silver, arranged in a tidy braided coronet atop her head. Her eyes were a tawny topaz, revealing intelligence and something else that strangely seemed to be disgust. Her lips, dark and rosy and eminently kissable, were pulled into a tight, disapproving frown.

"So, you've finally arrived," she said. Her voice was soft and throaty, but there was an edge to it Dylan didn't like.

"Everybody certainly seems concerned about punctuality around here," he complained.

Julianna hated the insolent way this unwelcome stranger was looking at her. Against all rules of propriety, his eyes were sweeping over her, from the top of her head to the tip of her shoes, lingering on her face, her mouth, her breasts, her hips.

It was, she considered furiously, almost as if she were some piece of property he was considering purchasing. Refusing to let him get away with such behavior, Julianna decided to show this uncouth barbarian that she could give as good as she was getting.

She didn't immediately answer his complaint as her own gaze swept over him, submitting him to an appraisal just as thorough as the one forced upon her.

Clad in the bright orange jumpsuit worn by terran transport pilots, and looking every bit as fierce as the men of his breed, he was tall with broad shoulders and a glistening spill of too-long black hair.

His deep-set eyes were a dark, rich blue and sparked with both irritation and an intelligence Julianna was not accustomed to seeing in men of his disreputable profession. His complexion was dark, like her brother's, and his cheekbones were a sharp, rugged slash. His unsmiling lips were full and sensual, but like everything else about this renegade, decidedly masculine.

As her gaze lingered on his mouth, without warning, Julianna experienced a sudden, unbidden and decidedly un-Sarnian curiosity about how those lips would feel on hers.

"I think you've mistaken me for someone else," he said on a smooth, rich voice. The corners of those sulky lips curved upward in unmistakable masculine amusement.

"Oh, I know exactly who you are."

Julianna was furious at herself when she realized he'd caught her staring at his mouth. Only the knowledge that terrans were as mindblind as she was kept her from being humiliated by her rebellious curiosity. Fortunately, there was no way he could have known what she'd been thinking.

She held out her hands, revealing the steel bands that encircled her wrists. "You're the man who's come to escort me to my execution."

His mind was still pondering that flash of unwilling desire he'd seen in her eyes. Such masculine preoccupation caused her icy words to take a moment to sink in. When they did, Dylan was certain that he must have misunderstood.

"Excuse me?"

"For what?" she inquired, suddenly looking as confused as he. "Doing your duty?"

Dylan tried again. "I meant, would you please repeat what you just said."

"About doing your duty?"

"No. The other. About why you believe I've come."

"Oh, that." Her expression hardened. Her tawny eyes were chips of amber ice. "I merely pointed out that I know you are the transport pilot we have been waiting for. The man the Elders have hired to take me to Australiana."

"You're kidding." Dylan arched a black brow. "You're being sent to Australiana?"

He remembered Starbuck telling him how, although Sarnia was a planet based on law and logic, there were those whose biomental systems went awry, causing them to act in ways considered a threat to the group.

When that happened, such people were quickly removed from society and if the psychological mind-altering drugs did not solve the problem, they were deported to the moon Australiana, where they, and others like them, were doomed to spend the rest of their lives in exile.

"Since I fail to see anything humorous about the situation, I could not possibly be kidding about such a thing," Julianna said stiffly. "And although Australiana is the alleged destination, I also know that it is your duty to see that I do not reach the colony alive."

Frustrated and confused, and wondering if somehow the scattered molecules of his brain had gotten put back together in some fashion that had rendered him hopelessly stupid, Dylan still couldn't understand what Starbuck's sister was accusing him of.

"You honestly believe that I'm going to kill you?" He gave her a look that suggested he thought she'd lost her mind.

"Oh, I don't believe that you will commit such an act, personally," she said with a calm that Dylan found especially irritating.

"Not when you have an entire ship of roughneck Janurian warriors under your command, who would forego a year's pay for the privilege of committing legalized murder."

Frustrated, Dylan raked a hand through his dark hair. "Look, lady—"

"The sun is going down," one of the guards interjected, cutting off his planned reply.

Dylan turned on him. "So what?"

"It is the wish of the Elders that the prisoner be off the planet before Truthfest begins," the other guard pointed out. "You have no time for such idle conversation."

Personally Dylan did not consider being accused of being a cold-blooded murderer, *idle conversation*. He intended to get this straightened out. Right now.

"Screw the Elders," he ground out.

It was obviously a highly unacceptable thing to say. The two guards' eyes, mere slits beneath that leathery ridge of their forehead, widened. Even Julianna gasped. It was only a slight exhalation of breath, but easily heard in the sudden stillness of the room.

Before he could continue arguing with Starbuck's sister, Dylan found himself facing two very lethal weapons.

"You may be foolish enough to disregard the mandate of the Ruling Council," the first guard said. "But we have families and a good life here on Sarnia. And we do not wish to be banished to some barren outback."

He waved the laser gun toward the door. "It is our duty to see that you and the prisoner are off the planet before the moon rises. And that is exactly what we intend to do."

"Let me get this straight. Are you actually telling me to get out of town before sundown?" Dylan asked dryly.

"That is exactly what we are telling you," the second guard agreed.

When it appeared that his sarcasm had flown right over the man's leathery head, Dylan decided that irony and sarcasm must be too complex a concept for the Janurian mind.

"Your ship is at the docking site. I have been informed by your second-in-command that the crew has it ready to leave."

Dylan swore and shook his head, trying to rid it of this ridiculous conversation. What was he supposed to do now? He still had no idea what was going on. He also had absolutely no idea how to begin to pilot a transport ship, whatever that was.

"I suggest we leave," Julianna murmured in that cool unflappable tone he was beginning to hate. "Unless you intend to end up a prisoner yourself. Or worse."

Crashing some damn spaceship trying to leave a planet he hadn't even known existed three weeks ago was a decidedly unappealing prospect. But from the expressions on the guards' bulldog-ugly faces, Dylan had an uncomfortable idea that there were worse fates. And these two thugs would undoubtedly be happy to show him a few of the more unsavory ones.

Despite his worldwide reputation for scientific genius, Dylan had never been a typical computer nerd. On the contrary, he had always appreciated the same things other, less intellectually gifted men enjoyed: an ice-cold beer on a hot summer day, a warm, willing and enthusiastic woman in his bed, and, of course, sports. Indeed, he'd had season tickets to the New England Patriots games for years and until this winter, when he'd been working overtime on his time-travel machine, he'd never missed a home game. And if there was one thing all those years of football games had taught him, it was that sometimes, when a carefully planned play went hopelessly awry, a guy just had to punt.

If these armed goons thought him to be a transport captain, that's just what he'd have to pretend to be. For now.

"Well, then," Dylan decided with a shrug, "I guess it's time we got this show on the road."

They were escorted by the four guards to a nearby air shuttle that reminded Dylan vaguely of Charity's Jeep Cherokee. Except that when the driver—also clad in the black uniform he now knew to be worn by the Janurian Guard—punched the ignition code into the dashboard computer, the vehicle lifted upward, hovering a few feet above the ground. The driver pressed the accelerator and the shuttle took off. Dylan could watch their progress on the computerized map.

The ride to the docking station took less than five minutes. Although when he'd first decided to take

Starbuck's place, Dylan had been filled with curiosity about this faraway planet that in his time was still unknown to Earth's astronomers, he paid scant attention to the foreign scene flashing by the darkly tinted windows.

Instead, his mind was on this unplanned dilemma. He reminded himself that all his life he'd been declared brilliant. After all, hadn't every university and think tank in the country—the world, actually—been after him since he was twelve years old? Hadn't he graduated from medical school at eighteen, before going on to MIT to earn his doctorate in physics in two years?

Hadn't Starbuck told him that he would write a benchmark study of solar flare arousal, a concept that was still being taught in Sarnian astrophysical psychology classes two hundred years in the future?

Which was, Starbuck had assured him, quite a feat, considering the fact that Galileo, Copernicus, Newton, Darwin, Einstein, Prescott and Pournelle—a scientist yet unborn—were the only Earthlings who'd ever earned mention in the Sarnian textbooks.

And even then there were footnotes pointing out that these seven men were not considered representative of their species. They were, the textbook writers had felt it necessary to point out, highly exceptional.

And hadn't he, against all odds, managed to cross time and space to arrive here on Sarnia?

So, surely he could think up some solution to what was becoming, admittedly, a very sticky problem.

After all, it wasn't every day that he was required to save not only the life of the woman who would soon become his sister-in-law, but quite possibly, his own, as well.

There was a way out of this, Dylan assured himself. Now all he had to do was think of it.

WHILE DYLAN'S MIND WAS clicking away with the analytical methodology that had always served him so well, Julianna was watching him surreptitiously, once again surprised by what she was witnessing.

Everyone knew that transport pilots were near the bottom of the social pecking order. They were rugged individualists, men incapable of following the strict dictates of a rigid society. They were also absolutely incapable of loyalty.

But they did serve an important purpose. Admittedly more intelligent than the deadly Janurian warriors, they effectively carried out those unsavory duties the ruling class of Sarnia found distasteful.

Legend had them descended from a group of terran astronauts who'd turned to piracy when their own world had abandoned them during the brutal ozone wars that had raged throughout the galaxy a century earlier. Whether it was true or not, the men had done nothing to disprove those old tales.

For a price, they would take their battered transport ships anywhere, on any mission. They routinely made their way past Sarnian government blockades, smuggling contraband onto the planet, earning vast profits for their efforts. Ignoring Federation restraints and peace treaties, they ran weapons to neighboring warring worlds, often delivering to both sides during the same conflict.

These men had no basic beliefs, no values governing their behavior, no religion. Filthy lucre was their god, and those who survived the danger, could become very wealthy.

For as long as she'd lived, they had also operated the prison ships, and Julianna knew that such pilots were not above turning a blind eye to violence aboard those vessels. So long as they were well paid. As she suspected this man must have been.

But there was something about him—some basic decency she sensed in him—that was worlds apart from the rest of his kind. In some strange way, he reminded her of her brother.

But that was ridiculous. Bram Valderian—known to the civilized world as Starbuck—was the most brilliant man in several universes. He was also the kindest. The idea that this unsavory renegade could have anything in common with her brother was ridiculous.

That she could even think such a thing if only for that brief, fleeting moment—showed exactly how distressed she had become since her arrest.

It was not exactly that she was afraid of dying. She'd known the risk from the beginning. Besides, death on Sarnia was not a time for grief. It was, Julianna had always been taught, merely the natural order of things. The old giving way to the new.

But when her father had ceased to exist during the last solar revolution, Julianna had experienced a startlingly deep feeling of pain and an even stronger sense of loss that was so distressingly human she realized that she'd inherited more of her mother's terran traits than she liked to admit.

Still, she had never feared her own death. It was whatever came before that had her stomach tied up in a million knots.

Would this man instruct the deed to be done quickly and humanely? Or would he allow his brutal Janurian warriors to drag the torture out? Julianna had heard whispers of deeds so brutal they were almost impossible to believe.

But if these rumors of cruelty were true, Julianna was forced to wonder whether she possessed the strength to die bravely, with the Sarnian dignity that had been ingrained in her since birth.

Would she, she worried, lose her carefully nurtured control, and behave like some emotional coward? Would she publicly weep as her mother had done in the courtroom? Would she tearfully crawl and grovel and beg for her life?

Such an undignified prospect was almost as unpalatable as the thought of impending torture. Which brought her turmoiled thoughts back to the large man seated beside her, and whatever plans he had in store for her.

As she watched his long dark fingers unconsciously rubbing his square, unyielding jaw, Julianna wished, for not the first time in her life, that she possessed Sarnian telepathy. What she would give to read this man's mind!

The shuttle came to a stop. Dylan shook himself out of his whirling thoughts and looked out the passenger window at a scene that could have been any waterfront district on Earth. The men lounging around looked as rough and dangerous as the neighborhood.

The only difference between this place and a Boston wharf was that instead of merchant ships lined up at the docks, huge vehicles that could have come from the special effects department of a *Star Wars* movie loomed over the moving walkway.

"Whatever you do," Dylan murmured, his voice low, for Julianna's ears alone, "just keep your mouth shut and follow my lead."

"I don't exactly have a choice, do I?" Despite her fear, her eyes, as they locked with his, revealed her blatant disdain.

Starbuck had described his sister as being unfailingly cool and calm and logical to a fault. From the way he had insisted that she never, under any circumstances, displayed irritation or frustration, Dylan suspected that he would have been amazed to see such open rebellion in Julianna's gaze.

Not that he could really blame her, Dylan decided. That she still thought him to be someone else was obvious. That she hated him was even more obvious, which wasn't all that surprising, since she believed he was planning to have her killed.

Still, Dylan found himself looking forward to her abject apology when she learned the truth.

He'd only make her grovel a little bit. After all, from what he'd been able to glean of the situation thus far, she'd already been through a lot.

Unbidden, images of a humble Julianna flashed through his mind. Julianna gazing adoringly up at him, her wide amber eyes glistening with tears of regret, her slender trembling hand—free of its steel restraints—pressed against his chest, her soft, throaty voice wavering only slightly as she begged him to tell her what she could do to make amends for her horridly misplaced distrust.

"I'll do anything," she murmured huskily, her hand moving slowly up his shirt. Her fingers played seductively with the dark strands of hair brushing his collar, leaving sparks against his neck. Her lips, slightly parted and enticingly pink, were only a whisper away from his. "Absolutely anything." Dylan felt his body respond to the gilt feminine invitation shimmering in her thickly lashed eyes.

The erotic image could have lasted a second, a minute or an eternity. And then, just when he felt rooted to the spot, it vanished like a puff of smoke.

As he focused his gaze on her pale face, Dylan was startled to see that Julianna appeared no less affected. Her eyes were wide and clearly startled. In them he thought he could read a lingering, unwilling desire.

Was it actually possible that she had read his mind? No, he remembered, Starbuck had assured him that Julianna was mindblind.

But damn it, somehow, she'd known what he was thinking. And she'd found the sensual image as appealing as he had. Dylan would have bet his laboratory and six months of funding on it.

Unable to resist the lure of her creamy skin, he reached out and ran his knuckles down her cheek. Her complexion was as white as floating snowflakes. And just as soft.

"Oh, you always have a choice, Juls," he answered her earlier rhetorical question. "It's what you do with that choice that makes the difference."

He flashed her the dazzling, woman-killing smile that occasionally, whenever he would remember to use it, worked wonders on females of all ages. "But I'd advise you not to make any waves until I get this little misunderstanding cleared up. No point in riling the natives."

He touched her one more time, just a hand to her hair, the gesture meant to reassure. And then he was out the door, standing beside the shuttle, waiting for her to follow.

If Julianna had been distressed by thoughts of impending death, she was terrified by the way such a gentle, unthreatening touch had left her quaking.

With her hands chained together in front of her, her balance was disturbed just enough to make climbing down from the shuttle difficult. Sensing her dilemma, Dylan reached up, caught her by the waist and lifted her easily to the ground.

Although she tried to tell herself it was only her imagination, Julianna would have sworn she could feel the heat of his touch through the material of her gown. Unbidden warmth rose in her cheeks, blazing like moonfire. Why, she was actually blushing, she realized. For the first time in her life.

"Oh, one more thing," Dylan murmured as they followed the armed guards down the moving sidewalk. "Your brother sends his love."

3

"MY BROTHER?" When one of the guards glanced back over his shoulder, she lowered her voice. "You've talked with Starbuck? How? Is he safe?"

"He's fine." Dylan too noticed the guard's sudden interest. "But it's a long story. I'll tell you all about it, later."

"I want you to tell me what you know about my brother, now. Because, in case it's slipped that less than agile terran mind of yours, I won't be alive, later."

"Damn it."

Frustration made Dylan rash. Forgetting that he hadn't wanted to draw any undue attention to their conversation, he stopped, caught hold of Julianna and spun her toward him. This time his fingers, as they curled around her upper arms, were far from gentle.

"I'm only going to say this once," he ground out. "So, listen very carefully, Julianna. Your brother told me that you were an intelligent woman, and since I had no reason to doubt his claim, I'm going to have to take his word for it.

"But, for an intelligent woman, you seem to have an unfortunate knack of jumping to conclusions. Which only makes for some very uncomfortable landings.

"I have no intention of killing you. Neither do I intend to let anyone else lay a hand on you.

"And, although you probably find this difficult to believe, I am no more pleased about this situation than you are. So, for now, until I can come up with a plan, I want you to stop thinking of me as the enemy. I also want you to keep that gorgeous mouth shut. Understand?"

No. She didn't understand any of this. But one look at his dark glower told her that this was not the time to argue. He had not raised his voice much above a whisper, but his brusque tone was uncomfortably hard. And final.

On top of that, he was standing so close. Too close. The tips of his dark leather boots were touching the toes of her shoes; she had to tilt her head back to look up at him. She could feel the power radiating through him and realized that this was not a man to be crossed.

Refusing to give him the idea that she was a submissive sort of woman—even on the eve of her death—yet not quite daring enough to challenge him in such a public forum, Julianna mumbled something that could have been an agreement. Or an oath.

"You know, Juls, you're definitely not at all what I expected." His left hand released her upper arm to curve around the back of her neck.

His fingers, stroking her sensitive skin, were causing havoc with her senses. And his blue eyes, as they moved slowly over her face, had nearly as much impact as if he'd placed one of those large dark hands on her breast. Julianna could feel her heart pounding; her mouth had gone as dry as sand.

This renegade was definitely not healthy for whatever little peace of mind she'd manage to salvage since her arrest.

Julianna would have jerked away from his light embrace, but realized that by doing so, she would be admitting his unsettling effect on her. Instead she stood her ground.

"You are precisely what I expected." It was a blatant lie, which went against every tenet of Sarnian society.

Lying was extremely uncommon behavior for a Sarnian. It wasn't that there was any specific moral prohibition, per se, but the Ancient Ones, in the Book of Laws, had correctly pointed out that one lie inevitably led to another until soon the entire situation had become untenable.

Reason was truth, the elders had written. *Truth, reason. All else was irrational.*

Starbuck had always insisted that hedging the truth on occasion, under proper circumstance, was not that irrational a solution. Determined to be a proper Sarnian, Julianna had never stooped to such behavior.

Until now.

"Oh?" Dylan asked. "And what, exactly, were you expecting?"

"An ugly, dark-hearted barbarian. A rogue. A man without scruples. Or conscience." When his thumb brushed against the hollow of her throat, Julianna wondered if he could feel the increased beat of her pulse.

Dylan could. "Ugly?" His fingers idly followed the neckline of her gown.

He'd always known that he was no Patrick Swayze, but over the years a satisfying number of women had professed to find him attractive.

"Do you really find me ugly, Julianna?" He sounded more amused than affronted.

"I find you unbearably so." Another lie. Only the second of a lifetime.

Once again, he surprised her. Throwing back his dark head, Dylan released a deep, booming laugh.

"Ah, Juls," he said, giving her a generous smile, "just think, of all the gin joints in all the universes, I walk into yours." The smile turned into a dazzling grin that left her momentarily spellbound. "I can tell that this is going to be one helluva trip."

Seeing that the guards had stopped and were watching them with undisguised interest, and a disturbing amount of male lust, Dylan sighed.

"Back to the business at hand." Hardening his tone, he commanded a guard to release Julianna's wrist restraints. "Stick with me, kid," he said once she was freed. "We'll get out of this mess, yet."

Against all logic, she was intrigued. Against every vestige of common sense, she was fascinated. Giving up trying to understand this man—including the strange, dizzying way he made her feel—Julianna continued walking with him toward the huge black transport ship docked nearby.

He'd expected the ship to resemble a cargo ship back home on Earth, the kind that crowded into Boston Harbor—big and bulky. But this one was sleek and lean and looked like the kind of spaceship Darth Vader would have flown around the *Death Star*. Dylan decided that the ship's sleek lines undoubtedly allowed it to slip past sensors on smuggling runs.

"The *Mutiny?*" Dylan asked with an arched brow as he read the name painted on the side of the craft.

"Transport captains are not exactly always law-abiding," Julianna pointed out stiffly.

"That much I've figured out for myself."

It was not going to be easy, Dylan knew. But, perhaps, it wasn't going to be all that difficult, either. He took one look at the uniformed human standing at the open door panel of the wicked-looking black ship and realized that intelligence was not a prerequisite for members of a transport crew. The ill-fitting orange uniform had not been cleaned or pressed anytime in the recent past.

"Where is Captain Kirkian?" the hatchet-faced officer asked with a suspicious glower.

"He got drunk, started a brawl in a tavern and got his ass thrown in the brig," Dylan answered easily, deciding that merchant sailors were undoubtedly the same throughout any universe. "Since the Ruling Council decreed that the prisoner must be off-planet by the start of Truthfest, there wasn't time to sober him up. So, I was hired in his place. I'm Captain Prescott."

As he'd hoped, the man took his words at face value. "The crew has prepared the ship for departure, Captain. I am First Officer Jack Turley."

Dylan took heart in the fact that his first officer's salute was every bit as sloppy as his uniform. He would not present much challenge.

He also wondered if all terrans, as humans were referred to on this planet, were of such poor stock. If this man was any example of the rest of his race, that would certainly explain why the ruling Sarnians considered them inferior.

It might also explain why Julianna would consider him capable of the cold-blooded, unfeeling acts she'd accused him of planning.

"Lead the way to the bridge, mister," he said, snapping a brisk salute that would have made a member of the Joint Chiefs of Staff proud. "We'll be right behind you."

The man's startled gaze went from Dylan to Julianna, then back to Dylan. "You are taking the prisoner with you? To the bridge?"

"Of course." Dylan gave him a cocky I'm-the-captain-and-can-do-whatever-I-want smile.

"But she's a female."

"You're very observant, Mr. Turley. Remind me to make a positive notation of that in your personnel file."

"But Captain Kirkian never allows females on his bridge," the officer argued. "Says they're bad luck."

"Considering his current circumstances, Captain Kirkian appears to be quite capable of making his own bad luck," Dylan pointed out. "Personally, I've never been superstitious."

The man continued to stand like a boulder, blocking their forward progress. "The crew is," he warned.

"The crew," Dylan said sharply, "is under my command. As such, they are expected to do whatever I tell them to do. Is that clear, mister?"

A dark red flush rose from the rumpled orange collar. "Yes, sir," the man mumbled.

"Fine." Dylan nodded his satisfaction. Giving Julianna an encouraging smile behind the first officer's back, he began walking down the narrow hallway. Behind them, the air-lock panel to the outside slid silently closed.

"Did the captain really get drunk?" she asked under her breath.

"Beats me," Dylan said with a shrug.

"Are you saying that you don't know where he is?"

"I haven't a clue."

Julianna had always considered herself tall. But this man's legs were a great deal longer than hers. She had to hurry to keep up with his long strides. "Then he could show up here at any time?" she whispered disbelievingly.

"I'd say that's a very good possibility," Dylan allowed. "All the more reason not to dally." Taking hold of her arm, he encouraged her to walk even faster.

"Are you taking over command of the ship?"

"Of course not. Don't worry, Juls, we're not going anywhere. I'm just buying time to figure out some way to get us out of this predicament."

His words, as unexpected as they were, had the ring of truth, Julianna decided. "Who are you? Really?"

"Dylan Prescott."

The name rang a very clear and very loud bell. Julianna skidded to an abrupt stop and stared up at him. "You can't be!"

"Juls," Dylan said patiently, pulling her forward again, "you simply have to stop this habit of contradicting everything I say."

"But Dylan Prescott is famous. His name is legendary in scientific circles. Why, his study of solar flares arousal is required reading at the Science Institute."

"That's what your brother told me," Dylan agreed with obvious self-satisfaction.

"Did Starbuck also happen to mention that Dylan Prescott lived more than two hundred years ago?"

"Yep." He flashed her another thousand-watt grin. "Ever hear of time travel, Juls?"

"Of course," she snapped. In her frustration, she forgot every bit of Sarnian composure she'd worked so hard to acquire over the years.

"Well, you just happen to be looking at the guy who wrote the book."

He was insane, Julianna decided grimly as they followed First Officer Turley through another narrow air lock onto the bridge of the transport ship's control module. That was the only possible answer. This man was even more dangerous than she'd first thought. Because if he actually believed himself to be Dylan Prescott—and it certainly appeared that he did—he was obviously a raving lunatic.

The bridge was as neat and tidy as that of the starship *Enterprise*. Which wasn't all that surprising, Dylan considered, since clutter would be potentially dangerous. Any small objects left unsecured would start floating around in Zero-G and cause damage to the ship's delicate machinery.

A uniformed officer approached and snapped a salute far brisker than the one Dylan had been treated to earlier. "Second Officer Cyborg 714 reporting that the ship is ready for departure, Captain, sir."

Dylan opened his mouth to tell him that there would be a delay in departure when another android turned from a communications console and said, "Captain, I'm receiving input from the port master."

Only Julianna, who was watching him intently, noticed Dylan's slight grimace. "Ignore it."

"But, Captain, it's a priority-one message. If you do not respond, netcom will automatically pick up the transmission and send it on to the fleet commander."

That was the last thing Dylan wanted. Ignoring Julianna's sharp glance, he said, "Well, then, let's have it."

The big screen on the wall filled with the frowning visage of a large, obviously vexed middle-aged man wearing a blue uniform and a great deal of gold braid on the brim of his hat.

"Good evening," Dylan said pleasantly. "What can we do for you?"

"This is the port master, calling the captain of the transport ship, *Mutiny*," the gruff voice announced.

"You've got him," Dylan said. "What's the problem?"

"The problem is that I have, in my outer office, another man who claims to be the captain of the *Mutiny*."

"You do?" Dylan exchanged a glance with Julianna, ignoring the interested muttering from several of the Janurian crewmen. "Congratulations. Let me be the first to commend you, Port Master."

"Commend me for what?"

"For being the one to apprehend an escaped prisoner, of course."

There was a moment's hesitation. "An escaped prisoner?" the man echoed.

"Captain Kirkian was arrested for becoming intoxicated, disturbing the peace and threatening the harmonic celebration of Truthfest," Dylan repeated the tale he'd told First Officer Turley.

"If you contact the Ruling Council, you'll discover that I was chosen to replace him on this very important mission." It was a dangerous bluff, but Dylan knew he had no choice but to try it.

Unfortunately, the man was proving less gullible than Turley. "That's not the way Captain Kirkian tells it."

"Of course not. After all, how anxious would you be to spend Truthfest in the brig?" Dylan countered. He turned to the communications cyborg. "Would you please contact the head of the Council of Elders and inform him that the port master needs proper confirmation of their order?"

"Oh, that won't be necessary," the official said quickly. "I would not want to disturb such an important individual right before the opening ceremonies."

"You are a wise man, Port Master," Dylan said. "And a true gentleman. I am certain that when you turn the escaped prisoner over to the proper authorities, you will receive suitable commendation." Dylan smiled. "In fact, I will send a com-memo detailing your act of patriotism, myself."

"Thank you, Captain Prescott." The man preened visibly. "You're cleared for takeoff, *Mutiny*. Safe journey to you and your crew."

"Thank you. And Good Truthfest to you."

Dylan rubbed his chin as the screen darkened. He had two choices. He could remain here in port and risk the chance that the authorities, who would have no record of a Captain Kirkian's arrest, would board the ship and take both Julianna and him into custody.

Or he could, as he'd already done, trust his fate to the stars.

Dylan made his decision. "Officer Turley," he commanded, "I'm putting you in charge of our departure. I will be in my quarters, preparing my com-memo concerning our gallant port master."

Dylan had taken the chance that the first officer would enjoy an opportunity to pilot the ship himself. From the surprised yet pleased look on the man's ruddy face, he realized he'd guessed right.

"Yes, sir." Turley snapped his fingers at a Janurian guard who'd been hovering nearby. "Loton, take the prisoner below deck."

"Glad to." The man's bestial face cracked an expectant smile that made Dylan's flesh crawl and caused Julianna, standing beside him, to shiver visibly.

"The prisoner is coming with me," Dylan corrected.

"But, sir," Turley protested, "female prisoners are always turned over to the Janurians prior to departure. It is the custom."

From the naked lust in all the Janurian warriors' eyes, as they crawled slowly over Julianna's rigid body, Dylan understood the logistics of this custom all too well.

"Customs change." His arm slipped possessively around her waist. "As captain of the *Mutiny*, I'm hereby invoking my rights to claim this female."

That said, he hauled her close against him, so they were standing chest to chest, pelvis to pelvis, thigh to thigh. Before Julianna could utter a single sound of protest, before she had a chance to brace herself for what was coming, his head swooped down and his mouth was on hers.

Her gasp of shock strangled in her throat, her hands, still bound together, curled into fists against his chest. And then all she was aware of was heat. And power.

Without seeking permission, his firm lips molded hers to a shape he preferred. His mouth was hard and hot and hungry. His tongue invaded, creating reckless pleasure; his teeth excited, causing exquisite pain. White-hot flames began licking at the aura of restraint she'd always wrapped around herself like a protective cloak.

Sensations sharpened even as a soft misty fog clouded Julianna's mind. She could taste a brisk hint of mint and the stronger, almost bitter flavor of caffoid on his breath. A dark, Earthy masculine scent rose from his skin, seeping into her bloodstream like an inhaled drug, and all the while she could feel the heat of his hard body burning its way through her thin gown, scorching her flesh, creating a pulsating ache between her trembling thighs.

His teeth nipped her bottom lip, drawing a moan; when he filled his large hands with her breasts, not gently, her blood began to heat and swim. A thousand pulse beats were humming beneath her sensitized skin. The air was thick and heavy, crackling with energy like a pitch-black sky during an ion storm.

And then, as his wet tongue trailed a fiery path up the side of her arched neck, something changed. Fear and anger and need tangled gloriously as the turbulence in him became a raging storm within her.

Her fists uncurled; her fingers grasped the front of his flight suit. Hungry for his dark, mysterious taste, Julianna twisted her head, drawing his wicked, wonderful lips back to hers. Again and again.

She was insatiable, matching his power, equaling his passion. Reality slipped away, reason disintegrated. They could have been the only two people on the ship. The planet. The universe.

Through the smoky haze enveloping his mind, Dylan realized that once again he'd miscalculated. He'd planned this kiss to demonstrate his control over, not just the woman the crew believed to be his prisoner, but every man on the ship, as well.

Julianna had said that transport pilots were renegades—cruel, brutal rogues. That being the case, it had been imperative to make his point forcefully. Finally.

But he hadn't counted on Julianna Valderian being so damnably soft. He hadn't expected her to taste so impossibly sweet. And he definitely hadn't planned to ignite such a fire storm.

Although he'd sensed the hidden fires inside Julianna, never in a million years would he have expected her to be so uninhibited. Her moist mouth was hot and avid, her desperate demand as forceful as his need. Soft little sounds somewhere between a whimper and a sob escaped from between those succulent lips.

His control was slipping away; Dylan was finding it harder and harder to hold on to a coherent thought. When she pressed her womanly curves against him, moving in a restless, hungry way that was openly carnal, his body responded in kind, his erection thrusting painfully against the harsh metal zipper of the flight suit.

Erotic images of making love to Julianna Valderian flashed through his mind, each one hotter and more provocative, until he felt in danger of exploding.

Dylan had never considered himself a greedy man. But at this suspended moment in time, he wanted it all. He wanted to touch Julianna everywhere; he wanted to rip off her clothes and taste every inch of fragrant flesh.

He wanted to be inside her. He wanted to bury himself in her sweet wet warmth, so deeply that he could touch her womb; he wanted to ride her hard and fast and long until her skin was slippery and hot and she was crying out, begging for release.

Dylan was on the verge of doing exactly that when he remembered where he was, where they were, and pushed her a little away from him.

Such self-restraint cost him; his entire body was throbbing painfully and the vicious pounding in his head was worse than any hangover he'd ever suffered.

He was not the only one caught unaware by the emotions that had surged full-blown during that heated kiss. Julianna's complexion was as white as the snow that had been falling on Castle Mountain when he'd left Maine. The only color in her face was a slash of vivid scarlet on both high cheekbones. Her eyes were wide and dark and filled with a discomfiting mixture of shock and humiliation.

Reminding himself that the entire exercise, no matter how badly miscalculated, had been to display authority, he managed, with a valiant effort, to control both his ragged breathing and his expression.

"This woman prisoner is mine," he repeated. "Until we arrive at our destination." He was pleased when his voice sounded far steadier than he was currently feeling. "Any crew member who disagrees with the captain's right to claim a prisoner is free to leave the ship. Now."

Although he thought he saw some ill-masked resentment in a few of the Janurian warriors' unfathomable gazes, not one man spoke up in defiance.

"Fine."

Dylan nodded his satisfaction, appearing as if he'd expected no other answer. In truth, he'd worried that he was going to have a problem keeping these barbarians away from Starbuck's sister. And although there wasn't anything he wouldn't do for Charity's fiancé, the idea of fighting a duel with some outer-space Neanderthal had been less than appealing.

He threw his arm around Julianna's shoulder, pretending not to notice when she flinched. "The prisoner and I will be in my quarters," he announced. "And I do not wish to be disturbed."

He turned to First Officer Turley. "You may carry on, Turley."

That little matter taken care of, Dylan suddenly remembered that he had absolutely no idea where the captain's quarters were located.

He turned to one of the uniformed cyborgs. "It's going to be a long night and I expect to be needing some subsistence. Please bring food and drink to my cabin."

He waited a heartbeat, then said, "On second thought, the prisoner and I will accompany you to the mess so I can select my meal personally. Then we will all go to my quarters, where you will leave the food, then return to duty, here on the bridge."

The cyborg, displaying a bit of very human ego, visibly preened at have been selected to serve his commander personally. "Yes, sir. Whatever you wish, Captain."

As Dylan turned to leave the bridge, Julianna's feet seemed nailed to the floor and she remained standing where she was.

"Don't dally, wench," he ground out when he heard a less-than-respectful chuckle from somewhere in the room. "Or you will learn the unpleasant consequences of disobeying a transport captain."

As they left the bridge, Dylan's arm still possessively around her rigid shoulder, Julianna's head continued to spin from that fiery kiss.

She'd always prided herself on her restraint. Yet the moment his mouth had touched hers, a lifetime of steely self-control had disintegrated.

What dark, evil power did this man possess, she wondered shakily, that he could create such an instantaneous assault on her senses?

Her instincts had been right all along, Julianna realized. Whoever this man was, wherever he had come from, he was definitely dangerous.

4

THE FOOD, unfortunately, was the first familiar thing Dylan had discovered on this distant planet. Packaged in foil envelopes, obviously dehydrated, it reminded him of the type of meal he was forced to carry on longer backpacking trips. An obvious—and only—advantage was its lack of weight; an equally obvious disadvantage was its taste.

As he watched what appeared to be a twenty-second-century microwave reconstitute their meal, he realized for the first time why his future brother-in-law had rhapsodized so enthusiastically over take-out pizza and potato chips.

The cyborg put their meals on a tray, covering the plates with what appeared to be an aluminum hubcap to keep them warm. Dylan didn't think the effort would make much difference in the food's taste, but he appreciated the attempt.

As they followed the cyborg through narrow hallways, doors shushed open and closed, obviously operating on the command of concealed sensors.

Outwardly Dylan appeared calm, a commander utterly comfortable in his position as captain. But Julianna, who was watching him carefully, could sense his intense concentration as he searched out the location of those sensors. She also sensed that he was memorizing the maze of hallways in the same way a space cartographer would prepare to map the universe.

Although the captain of a transport ship possessed ultimate control over his troops, Dylan quickly discovered that his living quarters were far from luxurious. A final steel door slid silently open, revealing a narrow cubicle approximately ten feet by eight feet. He suspected that the average American jail cell was larger.

There was a narrow, uncomfortable-looking bunk against one wall. Studying it, Dylan was reminded of a speaking engagement he'd once made at the University of Southern California. The conference had lasted three days, during which time he'd met a fellow scientist from Copenhagen who'd recently left her work in artificial heart research to work as a medical ethicist.

At first, over drinks in the Los Angeles Biltmore cocktail lounge, he'd been attracted to her brilliant mind, a mind that rivaled his own.

An hour later, he was admitting that her mane of sleek blond hair, gorgeous face and amazingly voluptuous body possessed an equally strong attraction. Enough so that when the conference was completed, he'd quickly agreed to her suggestion that they take the train up the California coast. The bunk in their compact compartment on the Amtrak Coast Starlight had been every bit as narrow as this one, Dylan remembered. But they'd managed just fine. Better than fine.

"Your quarters suit you?" the cyborg inquired, noting the slow smile that had appeared on Dylan's face.

Dylan shook off the memory, reminding himself that this was no time to be engaging in woolgathering.

"They're adequate," he replied brusquely. "Put the food on the table, then leave us."

His surly rudeness was intentional. He could not risk the humanoid reporting back that their new captain possessed a soft streak. All it would take would be for one Janurian warrior to speculate that the female prisoner might be his for the taking after all, and the ship's name *Mutiny* could become a self-fulfilling prophecy.

The cyborg quickly placed the tray on a nearby table made of some plasticlike material Dylan couldn't recognize and backed obediently out of the room. The door shushed behind him, leaving Julianna and Dylan alone for the first time since his arrival on Sarnia.

"Would you please tell me what this is all about?" Julianna demanded.

Still shaken, she couldn't decide whom she was more furious at: this man who claimed to be Dylan Prescott, for initiating that hot, mindblinding kiss; or herself for responding to it.

"Just hold your horses, Juls. We'll get to the particulars when the time's right."

Dylan's wink only served to irritate her further. Julianna stiffened her back and jutted out her chin. "And I suppose you're the one who determines when the time is right?"

"Got it on the first try."

Julianna thought she detected a hint of laughter in his voice, then decided that she must have imagined it. No one with any sense at all could possibly find anything humorous in their situation.

She stood by the doorway, arms folded over the front of her gown, watching as he inspected the small quarters. He was thorough, she decided, watching his hands slowly moving over every inch of wall space. She'd give him that. She concluded that he was undoubtedly searching out hidden sensors.

Although Julianna doubted that any crew member would be so brazen as to attempt to spy on anyone as brutal as a transport captain, since surveillance was a way of life on Sarnia, she was forced to admit that the idea of some government official putting observation equipment aboard while the ship was in port was not impossible.

Once he'd completed his study of the walls, Dylan began on the few pieces of furniture, checking the trunk at the foot of the bunk, behind the drawers of the desk, inside the intercom. He worked with a deft efficiency she couldn't help but admire.

And although she was not accustomed to observing a man's physical features, as he unscrewed the halozite ring in the overhead light fixture, she couldn't help noticing that his fingers were long and dark and narrow. They were the hands of an off-planet artist, or musician, perhaps.

Remembering the strings those fingers had so creatively strummed inside her as they'd roamed her back, then held her hips with a virile male strength, Julianna once again felt an alien heat rush into her cheeks.

Utilizing a lifetime of willpower, she forced it down.

"Well, everything looks clean," Dylan decided. By the time he finally acknowledged her presence again, she'd managed to get both her unruly mind and body under control.

"You've no idea how that relieves me."

He lifted a brow. He rocked back on his heels and studied her. During his investigation, she'd managed to coat herself in enough ice to cover Jupiter.

Having sampled her heat, Dylan knew that the image she was projecting was a false one.

"We need to talk openly," he said mildly. "And we couldn't do that if we were bugged."

She belatedly noted that whenever he spoke to her, he spoke English rather than Sarnian. When she asked about that point, he shrugged and said, "Starbuck told me that your mother is an American. He also told me that you were the one who taught him to speak English, which, by the way, proved to be a big help when his ecumenical translator started conking out on him.

"Although," Dylan continued as he lifted the aluminum covers off their meals, "it would have been a big help if you'd taught him a few more idioms. But since he ended up in the wrong century whatever you taught him probably wouldn't have been much use anyway. Language being so fluid."

He frowned as he lifted a plate and took a sniff. "I have no idea what this stuff is, but since I'm starving, I'll have to chance it. Care to join me for dinner, Ms. Valderian?"

As if on cue, Julianna's mutinous body embarrassed her again when her stomach growled. She hadn't eaten for hours. And unlike him, she couldn't understand his disapproval of the food. It was, after all, standard Sarnian fare.

"I am hungry," she admitted.

"Terrific. We'll eat first, then talk. Which do you want?"

"Given the choice, I think I'd prefer the Olympian mushroom platter."

"Sure." Dylan studied both plates. "Which is that? The gray or the brown?"

"The gray."

Dylan appeared relieved at her answer. "Then I'll take the brown." He handed her the plate, then sat down on the bunk.

Julianna, opting for discretion, chose the chair at the desk.

They ate in silence, Julianna daintily, Dylan cautiously at first, then, although his brow furrowed in distaste, digging in in a manner that revealed he'd been every bit as hungry as she.

"Lord, what I wouldn't give for a cheeseburger," Dylan said as he put his empty plate aside.

"A cheeseburger?"

"It's a thick slab of grilled beef with cheese melted over the top on a sesame-seed bun. With lettuce and tomato and onion. And tons of mustard. The bright yellow kind. I never have figured out the appeal of that trendy brown stuff passing as mustard these days."

Deciding not to attempt to decode his words, Julianna merely stated, "Sarnians do not eat meat."

"That may be. But your brother sure caught on fast enough," Dylan countered. "By his second day on Earth, I think he was hooked on pepperoni pizzas."

Julianna felt herself echoing his unconscious smile. "You really do know my brother, don't you?"

"He's the reason I'm here. I came to tell you and your mother that he reached Earth safely and that he's fine."

"I don't understand why didn't he come himself."

Dylan leaned back against the wall and linked his fingers behind his head. Although she told herself that she wasn't at all interested, Julianna couldn't help noticing how the gesture caused the muscles in his arms to press against the orange nylon flight suit.

"As I said, that's a long story. I promise to fill you in on all the details after you tell me how you got yourself into this mess."

She wanted to trust Dylan. She had no one else she could trust, and it was becoming more and more obvious that he was telling the truth about knowing her brother. But just as she felt herself beginning to believe him, something unpalatable occurred to her.

"Are you holding my brother captive on Earth?"

His frown was quick, dark and definitely dangerous. "Of course I'm not. As much as he wanted to return here, at least one more time, he didn't want to risk not being able to get back to Charity."

"Charity?" Fluent in several off-planet languages, Julianna definitely understood the word. "What does being kind have to do with Starbuck's decision to remain on Earth?"

"Charity is my sister's name," Dylan explained. "My other two sisters are Faith and Hope, which might make you think my mother is old-fashioned, but she's actually a very modern woman.

"Unfortunately, she turned awfully Victorian when she named her children. Prudence and Modesty were next on her list, but she ran out of girls.

"Not that she was going to let that stop her. I was supposed to be called Loyal until my father put his foot down and claimed the right to name his only son, which was damn lucky for me, don't you think?"

What Julianna thought was that Dylan Prescott's smile dispensed charm like the candy machines she remembered from her one trip to Earth.

The occasion had been the quatercentenary of her mother's homeland and although four hundred years of a nation's existence was a mere blink of an eyelash to Sarnians, the Americans, her mother included, seemed to have considered it quite an accomplishment.

Although she'd only been a child at the time, pleasant memories lingered. She'd first encountered the candy machine at some fantastical kingdom terrans had inexplicably named Disneyland. Her mother had put a silver coin into a slot, pressed a primitive type of lever and out had popped a round, sweet pink-and-white nugget that had exploded like laughter on her tongue.

"So Dad named me Dylan," he continued, oblivious to Julianna's thoughts. "After the poet, not the folksinger.

"Charity saved Starbuck's life," Dylan said. "After he landed on Castle Mountain during a blizzard."

She recognized the name immediately. It had flashed across the computer screen an instant before her brother had disappeared from his laboratory. And his planet.

"Castle Mountain, Maine?"

"That's it. Charity's police chief there, and she found him lying unconscious in the snow on her way home."

"Your sister is a law-enforcement officer?"

As an xenoanthropologist, Julianna knew that women on other planets had achieved varying degrees of equality to their male counterparts. Still, she couldn't personally imagine dealing with criminals on a daily basis.

Although no self-respecting Sarnian would ever think of breaking the law, there was a constabulary on the planet to keep the more emotional and sometimes violent immigrants from other planets in line.

"Starbuck couldn't believe that a woman was psychologically or physically equipped to do such a potentially dangerous job," Dylan revealed agreeably. "Until he got a chance to watch Charity in action."

"You should have seen the riot he caused when he beamed himself into this tacky waterfront bar and tried to interfere in a dispute between a bunch of alleged lobster poachers.

"Of course, Charity insisted she had things under control, and knowing her, she probably did, but your brother took one look at her surrounded by those enormous, angry, drunk men and all hell broke loose."

"Are you saying that my brother actually engaged in physical violence?" Julianna asked unbelievingly. "In a tavern?"

"It was a regular donnybrook," Dylan said with a wide grin of remembrance. "Unfortunately, I got there a little too late to participate, but from several eyewitness accounts, he barely lifted a finger and managed to knock those guys out.

"In fact, according to the bartender, the only proof he'd moved at all was the sight of them crumpling to the floor unconscious, one after the other, like falling timber."

"Tal-shoyna," Julianna murmured.

Her brother had studied the Sarnian martial art form for years, alleging that he'd appreciated the way it stressed mental rather than physical control over an adversary. But she knew that there was a seldom discussed, darker side to the ancient martial arts method, as well—a movement that, if not carefully controlled, could break an opponent's neck quickly and cleanly.

Julianna couldn't imagine her brother ever, under any circumstances, resorting to such violence.

"That's what he told me later," Dylan said cheerfully. "And although you could tell that he was feeling pleased as punch with himself, Charity was as furious as I've ever seen her. For a minute, I was afraid she was going to toss Starbuck in the clink and throw away the key."

Since her head had begun to ache, Julianna decided to deal with such an outlandish scenario later.

"Starbuck was supposed to be going to Venice," she revealed. "But something went wrong at the last minute. I called out to him that he was on target for some place called Castle Mountain, but he was gone before we could reset the coordinates. The computer searched and searched for him, but we couldn't find anything."

"That's probably because that same little glitch landed him two centuries ahead of time. I'm pretty sure it was the solar flares that got him off course," Dylan said.

"But he and Charity seem to think that he was mentally drawn into her romantic fantasy. Whatever, they hit it off right away, and the rest, as they say, is history."

"Are you saying that your sister, Charity, is the reason Starbuck did not return home to Sarnia?"

"That's exactly what I'm saying."

He rewarded her with another of those warm smiles. Julianna steeled herself against letting it affect her.

"But whatever his reason for landing where and when he did, it definitely turned out to be a lucky glitch. Starbuck and Charity are getting married," Dylan divulged.

The words hit Julianna like a meteor shower. "Married? Surely you don't mean bonded?"

Starbuck having a dalliance with a terran woman, Julianna could accept. After all, her brother had always displayed a distressingly un-Sarnian-like sex drive that she'd suspected was a direct result of his human genes.

But to defy convention by bonding himself to a terran would do irreparable damage to his career. Something he'd always valued dearly. And although her brother may be unconventional, he wasn't a Haldon-headed idiot.

"I mean *married*." Dylan's deep voice broke into her unbelieving, whirling thoughts. "Like in man and wife. For better or worse. For life."

"But Starbuck is already bonded. To a Sarnian. And he would never break his word."

Starbuck had told Dylan something about his former fiancée. A superb product of genetic engineering, the woman he'd been promised to at age seven was blond, blue eyed and slender as a Genetian reed and, Starbuck had admitted, as frigid as the glacial plains of Algor.

"He didn't have to. From what I hear, Sela was the one who broke their bond promise after he lost his prestigious position at the institute."

Hearing Sela's name from this man's lips was yet additional proof that he knew her brother. Having him mention Sela's coldly self-serving behavior proved that he knew Starbuck quite well.

"Sela only behaved in such a manner because she resented the undue attention his work had attracted," Julianna argued. "His insistence on clinging to what the entire scientific community considered heretical beliefs also endangered her career as a Sarnian time-management professional.

"But Starbuck always believed that the rift was only temporary. He insisted that once he returned to Sarnia with proof that his theories were valid, Sela would put aside her objections."

"He may have thought so once," Dylan agreed mildly. "But believe me, Juls, once he met my sister, all bets were off."

In the space of less than two hours, she'd seen this man lie easily and often. But something in his expression told her that about this, at least, he was telling the truth.

"So he continued the tradition," she murmured, more to herself than to him.

"Of Valderian males marrying terran women? I suppose you're right."

Julianna was no longer surprised that Dylan knew of her parents' daring marriage. "I hope he and your sister are as happy as my parents were," she said softly.

Dylan watched the fond light warm the previously cold frost in her remarkable golden eyes. "They're crazy about each other," he assured her. "I can see them fifty years from now, helping their grandchildren build snowmen and women in the front yard."

Grandchildren. The idea of her brother choosing to marry a terran and remain on Earth had come as such a shock she hadn't even considered the idea of him having children with this Charity woman. But she realized that Earth women routinely chose to give birth to their own children, rather than utilize surrogates as Sarnian women had been doing for centuries.

Starbuck and Charity's child would make her an aunt. Something stirred deep inside Julianna. Something that brought both warmth and a strange, inexplicable yearning.

Dylan watched the shadow move across her eyes and decided not to probe too deeply. He knew, from his own personal experience, that the idea of Charity and Starbuck took time getting used to. Besides, there were more important things to discuss.

"So," he said, his expression turning as grave as she'd seen it thus far, "now that I've caught you up on the family news, why don't you tell me what the hell kind of mess you've gotten yourself into?"

She bit her lip. Although Dylan Prescott wasn't the brutish transport pilot she'd first thought him to be, it still wasn't easy sharing the most personal debacle of her life with a complete stranger.

"It's a bit complicated."

"Does it have anything to do with those documents you found defaming the Ancient Ones?"

Julianna had been taught from the cradle to conceal her thoughts and emotions. But she couldn't keep the shock from her face. "How did you know about that?"

"Starbuck told me. He also said that what you were working on was dangerous." He gave her a sober look. "It appears he was right.

"Starbuck is always right," Julianna said without rancor. She sighed.

Even as he reminded himself that he and Starbuck's sister were in a real pickle, that he needed to keep his mind on the business of extricating them from this mess, Dylan couldn't ignore the way the deep intake of breath lifted her soft breasts against the silvery bodice of her gown.

"It is true that during my research into our civilization's past, I discovered a packet of documents defaming the Ancient Ones."

"Starbuck told me that your ancestors were among the Ancient Ones," Dylan recalled.

"That's true. And our history reveres them for bringing peace and reason to a savage, uncivilized planet." She frowned at what she now knew to be a horrendous lie. "But among the documents I've discovered is a diary alleging that a vibrant, matriarchal society existed on Sarnia long before the arrival of our ancestors."

"Starbuck told me about that, too."

"He did?" She couldn't keep the surprise from her face.

"I told you, we're best friends," Dylan said. "And best friends share everything."

"Then you know that the diary claims the Ancient Ones came not in peace, but at the bequest of the husband of the Elder Mother, the planet's ruler."

"He mentioned something about that. I also reassured him that yours certainly wouldn't be the first society to fudge when writing its history books."

"True. But my documents prove that our entire system of belief and laws is based on a falsehood. The diary claims women ruled Sarnia in peace and prosperity for several centuries with a vision of equality for all until Elder Mother's husband took control in a quick but horribly bloody coup.

"And when it was over, to ensure that the females would not be allowed to reestablish their claim, members of the original ruling families were brutally killed. Or, in the case of children, banished to the moon Australiana."

"Which eventually became a penal colony for those individuals who could not adapt to the strict rules of Sarnian law," Dylan remembered Starbuck telling him. "A law based on logic and reason. And the unequivocal biological superiority of males."

Julianna nodded. "Yes."

"If that's true, it is a bit different from what Starbuck told me about Sarnia's past," Dylan allowed. "But your brother wasn't certain that you've proven the diary's authenticity."

"Since his departure, I have managed to prove that it is legitimate."

"How?"

"The diary allegedly belonged to Elder Mother's youngest granddaughter, who escaped the purge when the household majordomo dressed her in servant's garb and passed her off as her own daughter. They were in the group that was banished.

"I used a technique similar to your own carbon dating. The diary was written during the five-year period after the Ancient Ones and Elder Mother's husband seized Sarnia."

"What about the letters?"

"The ones alleging that Elder Mother's husband, with assistance from our ancestors, initiated a bloody purge to gain absolute control?"

Dylan nodded.

"They are also authentic. They were written on the material used on the Ancient Ones' original planet, and they detail the plan quite thoroughly."

"But why would they want to help some thug take over an entire planet?" Dylan, always the scientist, had learned never to accept anything at face value.

"There were two reasons documented in the correspondence. One was that they'd created a sort of doomsday weapon they wanted to test. A weapon that would ensure peace because the other worlds, dreading the deadly consequences, would be too afraid to declare war upon them."

"But Starbuck told me that your planet has been peaceful for all these centuries because of the higher intelligence of its people."

"That undoubtedly has something to do with it," Julianna allowed. "But whispered rumors of our secret Sarnian weapon of annihilation have persisted throughout the centuries. So far, no other planet has dared test those rumors."

"Talk about your cold war defense politics," Dylan muttered. "You said there was another reason?"

"Yes. The Ancient Ones had destroyed their planet with unchecked pollution. As luck would have it, they were actively seeking some place to move their population when Elder Mother's husband made his inviting offer."

He whistled softly. "You were sitting on a virtual powder keg. Starbuck was worried that if anyone at the institute discovered what you were working on, you could be arrested for heresy. Or treason."

"That's precisely what happened. I had planned to release the data during Truthfest."

"Nice timing," Dylan said dryly, thinking how such a bombshell would definitely put a damper on the planet's annual festival.

"I thought it would be logical," Julianna agreed.

"Did it happen to cross your mind that it would also be damned dangerous?"

"I had no choice. It was necessary to tell the truth."

Reason was truth. Truth, reason. All else was irrational.

Her entire belief system had been predicated on those laws, proscribed centuries earlier by the Elders. And even once she'd learned that they hadn't obeyed their own commands, Julianna had found herself bound to a deep-seated sense of honesty. And honor.

"Unfortunately, my most trusted assistant turned out to be a government spy and turned me in to the authorities before I could take the truth public."

Dylan knew Julianna Valderian was intelligent. And, having come to know her brother so well, he wasn't all that surprised to discover that she possessed an obvious stubborn streak. Having been accused of being irritatingly single-minded himself, especially when he was working on a particular piece of research such as his quantum jump time theory, Dylan could appreciate that aspect of her personality.

But he was surprised that she'd been so naive. No wonder Starbuck had been worried about his sister. It was obvious that she was yet another cockeyed idealist, like Charity, Dylan mused. Even after years spent on a big-city police force, dealing with hardened criminals, she still managed to see good in almost everything. And everyone.

Dylan had thought his sister would grow out of her naiveté, but since she was twenty-eight years old and still a wide-eyed optimist, he'd come to the conclusion that she'd probably never entirely throw away her rose-colored glasses.

Despite the fact that Charity was outwardly open, while Starbuck's sister was reserve personified, they had a great deal in common. With her brother galaxies away on Earth, Julianna obviously needed someone to watch out for her.

"So you were tried and convicted. And banished to Australiana," Dylan said, deciding that this was where he'd come in.

"Yes. But I know, with every fiber of my being, that the Ruling Council does not intend to let me live." Her voice held no fear, simply fact.

Dylan sighed. Obviously fate had elected him as the person destined to watch out for Julianna Valderian.

Julianna watched as Dylan sat on the bunk for a long, silent time, obviously considering his options. He was leaning forward, his elbows on his knees, his fingers linked between his legs.

Once again her attention was drawn to those lean, dark hands. Once again her unruly mind remembered how they'd created such heat deep within her body.

She'd never had a man touch her like that before. In truth, she'd never experienced the hot, dangerous thrill of a man's lips against hers. Categorically refusing to become chattel by donning the Sarnian marriage collar all female brides were required to wear, Julianna had planned to spend her life alone, dedicated to her work.

Well, she didn't have much time left. And now, after the havoc this man had caused, Julianna found herself wondering if she truly wanted to die without at least testing that unsettling phenomenon a bit further.

It was only logical, she told herself. After all, as an xenoanthropologist, such sexual experimentation would merely be part of her work. Wouldn't it?

"Well," he said finally, dragging those long fingers she found so appealing through his dark hair, "I suppose the next thing to do is decide how to break you out of this traveling jail before we get to Australiana."

Shocked by the idea of even attempting to escape, all thoughts of sexual experimentation fled her mind as Julianna stared at him. Before she could point out the fallibility in such skewed logic, there was a knock on the door.

Dylan stiffened, shot Julianna a warning look and pressed his finger to his lips, counseling silence.

"Enter," he called out.

The door slid open, admitting a stunning woman with a mass of thick red hair. Her slanted green eyes reminded Julianna of a Algorian polarcat. She was obviously not a genetically designed Sarnian.

Since the only logical reason for breasts was to feed a child, Sarnian women—who had utilized surrogates for the unpleasant task of childbearing for the past two centuries—no longer possessed them. This woman had full, rounded breasts the color of cream. They also appeared on the verge of spilling out of her deeply cut tunic. The abbreviated skirt of the tunic, Julianna considered with disgust, barely covered the essentials.

"I am Kala," the woman purred silkily. She entered the narrow cubicle on a feline glide, knelt down before Dylan and, without so much as a by-your-leave, pressed her hand against his chest. Her fingernails were as long as talons and painted a daring scarlet. "The captain's woman."

5

KALA'S BREATH WAS a soft warm breeze against Dylan's face. Her crimson-tipped hands moved to the zipper tab of the flight suit, her intent obvious. She was, without a doubt, the most physically perfect woman he had ever seen. An aura of sexuality surrounded her, enveloping him in a carnal cloud.

The zipper slowly lowered nearly to his waist. Her fingers teased a tantalizing trail through the dark arrowing of chest hair. When she pressed her palms against his chest, then moved them lower still, a distant part of Dylan's mind waited for the inevitable. But not a thing was happening. Nothing. Nada. Zip. He glanced down to confirm that his body wasn't sending false messages to his mind.

"Sorry, sweetheart," he said, plucking her talented hands from his body. "But, as you can see, this captain already has a woman."

The female humanoid glanced around, as if noticing Julianna for the first time. "I don't mind," she said without missing a beat. "Sometimes Captain Kirkian preferred more than one female."

"I don't." Gently he stood, lifting her to her feet.

A small pout formed lips created for a remarkable range of sensual tasks. "You don't like me?" She turned around slowly, revealing a body that was a *Playboy* centerfold, Las Vegas show girl and *Sports Illustrated* cover girl rolled into one. "But I was created specifically for terran pleasure."

"You're lovely," Dylan said, deciding that had to be one of the understatements of the century. Of the millennium.

But even if he had been aroused, the idea of making love with a humanistic machine that could have been constructed by an adolescently sexual male mind in some Hollywood special-effects department would have proven a distinct turnoff.

"I'm one of those conservative kinds of captains who prefer one female companion at a time." He gave Julianna a look rife with lusty intention. "And for now, I think I'll stick with the woman I've got."

The humanoid's judicious study of Julianna's slender, stiff body revealed what her computer brain, trained to believe herself to be the ideal female form, thought of that surprising idea.

But programmed never to refuse a terran male, the voluptuous cyborg gave Dylan a dazzling smile that would have put any Miss Universe contestant to shame.

"Perhaps later," she suggested silkily. "After you're finished with her."

As she tossed her fiery mane in Julianna's direction, the tinge of scorn lacing her throaty tones captured Dylan's unwilling interest. He'd dabbled a bit in artificial intelligence.

He wondered how advanced science had become in that respect. Was it actually possible that this computerized woman possessed human emotions? Such as jealousy?

Julianna watched Dylan studying that oversexed android and experienced a sudden urge to pick up the nearest object and fling it at his handsome dark head.

Even as her fingers curled around the empty dinner plate, reality came crashing down on her. What was she thinking of? Surely she wasn't jealous? Jealousy was, she reminded herself firmly, a distinctly un-Sarnian emotion.

But, she admitted reluctantly, it was also a very human one.

Kala ran her blood-red fingernails along the arch of Dylan's upper lip. "Any time you want me," she reminded him, her liquid gaze offering a myriad of sensual invitations, "I'm yours."

With one last scathing look in Julianna's direction, she exited on a slow swivel of lushly formed feminine hips, leaving Dylan and Julianna alone again.

"I'm sorry," Julianna said, not meaning the words for an instant, but believing that, for politeness's sake, they should be said.

Dylan, who was still pondering that very human emotion he'd viewed in Kala's green gaze and wondering exactly how her creator had taught her to think for herself, rubbed his chin thoughtfully. "Sorry?" he asked distractedly. "For what?"

"If you'd been alone, you could have had sex with that . . . Kala." Strangely, several other words had popped into her mind. None of them complimentary.

"What?" Dylan turned and looked at her with honest surprise. "Don't tell me you think that I'm so hard up for a woman that I'd feel the need to go to bed with a computer?"

"A very attractive computer," Julianna reluctantly pointed out. "I'm told that terran men find such voluptuous physiques irresistible. I've also heard that transport androids are programmed to possess inexhaustible passion, along with an overwhelming emotional need to please their human masters."

Dylan had thought he'd managed to overcome her negative opinion of him. Obviously, even though she no longer believed him to be a rogue transport pilot, she didn't think much of human males in general.

"Her design was appealing," he admitted. "And passion is always a plus, in its place. But I've always been extremely choosy about my female companions."

She arched a disbelieving blond brow. "I am surprised. I was brought up to believe—and my field studies have confirmed—that the average terran male is far from discriminating when it comes to his sexual partners."

A temper he seldom displayed flared. Dylan had a sudden urge to yank her into his arms and kiss that haughty, superior Sarnian expression right off her face. He resisted.

"When you get to know me a little better, Juls," he said, approaching her slowly, steadily, like a predator on the prowl, "you'll discover that I'm definitely not your average terran male."

He was standing too close to her again. Julianna could feel the heat radiating off him, creating warmth within her own rebellious body. It was like coming out of an Algorian ice cave into a blazing hot Australianan sun. It was also unreasonably unnerving.

She moved away until her back was literally and physically against the wall.

Knowing he was being obnoxious, but enjoying her obvious discomfort, Dylan leaned forward. "Regarding female physical attributes, I'm flexible. I've always believed that sex is ninety percent mental, anyway."

His steady gaze was holding hers with the sheer strength of his not-inconsiderable will. His eyes were blue, like the mountain lakes on Saxton, in the outer ring of the Tenth Stratum, but much, much darker. At the moment they reminded her of the storm-tossed seas on the planet Volcanian.

A woman could drown in such dangerous eyes, Julianna considered. And this very dangerous, unnervingly vital man probably wouldn't lift a finger to save her.

"To Sarnians sexual congress is always mental," she allowed through lips that felt as dry as Australianan silica sand.

His lips were scant inches from hers. "I said ninety percent," Dylan reminded her on a low, husky voice that ruffled her nerve endings.

She could feel his breath—warm and inviting and undeniably appealing—against her own lips. Lips that parted unconsciously.

"If you make the mistake of skipping that important ten percent, you're missing one helluva lot, Juls."

Against all reason, and totally against her will, Julianna felt a flutter in her stomach, like that of the gossamer-winged flitterflys on Evian 4.

She threw up her chin, hating the way she was finding his cobalt gaze, the shape of his mouth, the warmth of his breath, his predatory male behavior so hypnotic.

"I'll have to take your word for that."

"You do that," he agreed amiably. "For now. But first let me give you a little taste of what you've been missing."

Without stopping to so much as ask her permission, he tipped forward that last minuscule inch and brushed his lips against hers.

Unlike the earlier, hard, brutal kiss on the *Mutiny*'s bridge, a kiss that had been meant as an act of possession, a demonstration to the Janurian crew that he had claimed his prisoner, this time his mouth was as soft as the velvety petals of one of her mother's moonflowers.

Something that felt like liquid moonlight shimmered through Julianna, lighting her from the inside out. Before she could respond or reject, he pulled back.

Staring up at him, with curious, trembling fingers, she touched her lips, where an alien warmth still lingered.

"And for the record, even if Kala had been one hundred percent human female, I still would have turned her down. Because I've always preferred women who present more of a challenge."

He gave her another one of those warm, intimate, horrendously dangerous smiles and ran his finger down her slim, aristocratic nose.

"Women like you, Juls."

His words, his gaze, the lingering warmth invading her body had her lowering her lashes to conceal the confusion in her eyes.

"You shouldn't talk to me this way," she protested on a voice she wished was steadier. "It isn't proper."

"You mean it isn't Sarnian."

She lifted her gaze, surprised and admittedly relieved that he understood so quickly. Perhaps they could reach an understanding, after all. Perhaps she could regain her equilibrium.

Perhaps, Julianna thought dryly, she'd suddenly sprout wings and begin to fly.

"That's precisely what I meant." There. Her voice was much calmer. More self-assured. More coolly, properly Sarnian.

Unable to resist the lure of her silky skin, wanting to stop her before she'd managed to encase herself again in that ice she wore like a protective suit of armor, Dylan ran the back of his hand down her cheek and watched, both pleased and satisfied, as the soft color bloomed.

"But I'm not Sarnian," he reminded her needlessly. "And neither are you. Not entirely," he interrupted when she opened her mouth to quickly protest that allegation. "Let's not forget that your mother was every bit as human as I am. And Starbuck told me that human genes tend to be dominant in the offspring of terran/Sarnian parents.

"But don't worry, Juls, before this little adventure is over, I think you'll discover there are some definite advantages to possessing terran traits."

His meaning was as clear as quartzalite. When Julianna refused to answer, he gave her another quick, hard kiss that rocked her all the way to her toes. A kiss that ended much too soon.

"So, how long will it take this ship to get to Australiana?"

The abrupt change in topic momentarily caught her off track. Julianna wondered if Dylan's agile mind always leaped from subject to subject so quickly, and decided that from what she'd seen thus far, it must.

"Three days."

"Earth days? Or Sarnian days?"

Good point, Julianna allowed. A thought suddenly leaped unbidden into her mind. A rash, daring, entirely un-Sarnian thought. If Dylan Prescott was a brilliant as the history books alleged, and thus far he certainly seemed to be, why couldn't she use him to aid her cause? If any individual could figure out how she could escape her death sentence, return to Sarnia and resume her campaign for female equality, it was Dylan.

The appealing idea caused a little rush of excitement to skim up her spine, not unlike the one she'd experienced at Dylan's kiss.

"Although our times are not calibrated exactly the same, the circadian rhythm on Sarnia is much the same as that on Earth."

She assumed that Dylan, as a scientist, would know that experiments done both in tightly controlled laboratory conditions and outer space revealed that several species—humans included—reacted to a more or less regular cycle of activity.

"That is one of the reasons Starbuck chose Earth for his destination," she added.

"Then this ship's schedule has undoubtedly been attuned to that time."

"I would think so," Julianna agreed. "Means of creating an artificial day and night to accommodate such circadian rhythm is routine on space voyages."

"That definitely makes things easier. It also gives us plenty of time to come up with a plan."

She watched as he began rummaging through the desk drawers. "I believe that is trespassing."

"So sue me." He smiled grimly as he located the weapon he'd seen while searching the room. "Bingo."

She shuddered involuntarily as she watched him examining the laser pulsar. "We Sarnians disapprove of weapons."

"Tough." It didn't look that different from a regular handgun, Dylan decided. He could probably manage to use it, in a pinch. "In case you've forgotten, Juls, those papers you've discovered prove that your revered Sarnian nation wasn't exactly established by pacifists."

He pointed the weapon at the door, squinting slightly as he tested the sights. "Besides, if one of those ridge-headed goons decides to challenge the captain's claim and take you below decks, I have a feeling that you'll find this gun a great deal more appealing."

Remembering the cruel, lustful gleam in those Janurian warriors' eyes, Julianna knew that he was right. Since she was also loath to admit it, she remained silent.

"And now, although I hate to give you the impression that I'm not exactly Superman, I'm afraid I'm about to crash. Obviously this intergalactic traveling stuff takes something out of a guy."

"Are you saying you are fatigued?"

"I'm saying that I'm beat. So, as much as I'd love to solve our little problem right now, I've decided to sleep on it. Things will undoubtedly look more encouraging in the morning. They always do."

Having had more time to deal with her dilemma that Dylan had, Julianna doubted that.

"There is only one sleeping pallet," she pointed out.

"So?"

She stiffened her back. "So I have absolutely no intention of lying with you. Such behavior would be highly improper."

Not to mention incredibly dangerous, she tacked on mentally, not quite deciding whether it was Dylan Prescott she couldn't trust, or herself.

Dylan muttered a curse as he dragged his hands through his dark hair. "Believe me, Juls, even if I did have any sexual designs on you, right now I'm too damned beat to follow through."

That was possible. Still, in her studies of the terran species, she'd learned of the rapid recovery ability possessed by some males. And although she now noticed dark shadows under Dylan's eyes that she'd not previously been aware of, Julianna refused to surrender.

"As captain of this ship, the bunk is rightfully yours."

"We both know I'm not the damn captain."

"That is beside the point," she said stiffly. "The fact remains that the crew believes you to be the captain, and you are certainly behaving as the captain, so it is only logical that you are entitled to a captain's privileges. I will sleep on the floor."

Dylan muttered another low, virulent curse her knowledge of English language didn't cover. But the meaning was clear, nevertheless.

"The hell you will." He sat down on the floor and yanked off his boots. "I'll take the floor."

"But—"

He jabbed a finger at the narrow bunk. "You take the bed. That's an order from the ship's captain. Got it?"

The way he barked at her, Julianna felt a vague urge to return a brisk salute. She resisted. "If you're asking if I understand your meaning, that you are wielding your rightful authority as commander of this vessel, the answer is yes."

She was going to drive him crazy. Stark raving mad. He'd always thought his sister to be the most stubborn female he'd ever encountered. But Julianna Valderian could definitely give Charity a run for her money.

Dylan ground his teeth, making a mental apology to his parents, who'd paid a fortune for his youthful orthodontic work.

"Good. I'm glad we got that settled."

That said, Dylan put the laser on the floor beside him, turned off the light, then sprawled out, using his arm for a pillow.

"And don't worry, I have no intention of taking captain's privileges by raping you in the night."

"I never believed that you would. After all, you are obviously a friend of my brother's and if Starbuck thought there was even the most remote chance that you would harm me, he never would have sent you here to me in the first place.

"So, it would only be logical that you will exercise restraint when it comes to any untoward masculine physical impulses you might experience toward me during the night."

She waited for a response. Either an argument, or an agreement. But there was only the slow, steady sound of Dylan's breathing.

"Dylan?" she whispered into the darkness.

His only answer was a rough, ragged snore.

Against all logic, since she was not alone in the darkened room, Julianna had never felt so lonely.

She lay down on the hard narrow bunk, folded her arms across her chest, and waited for morning.

THE DREAM CAME. It was dark and she was all alone, out in the middle of a storm-tossed sea. Some distant memory reminded her that her father had taught her to swim. Indeed, Starbuck had once accused her of being part sea-creature, to which her mother had laughed and called her a mermaid.

But for some reason, on this dark and stormy night, her aquatic skills had deserted her. It was as if leaden weights had been tied around her ankles. Her wrists. She struggled and struggled, but her arms and legs grew more and more exhausted.

Icy waves washed over her, swamping her again and again. She saw black-gowned men standing on the shore, arms folded, expressions grim in the weak, stuttering crimson beam slanting downward from the sliver of cold, crescent moon.

She tried to call out for help but swallowed a mouthful of salty water. Though she struggled frantically against the rushing tide, she felt herself sinking deeper and deeper beneath the dark surface.

But, like her brother, Starbuck, Julianna had never been a quitter. With one last mighty effort, she pulled her head above the water. It was then that she recognized the men standing at the edge of the churning black surf. It was the Ruling Council of Elders. They were laughing, enjoying her distress, anticipating her death.

She shouted at them, then felt unseen tentacles curling around her bare legs, pulling her down, down far beneath the cold dark sea.

Dylan woke with a start at Julianna's screams. Leaping to his feet, he made it to the bunk in one long stride, gathered her into his arms and held her tight.

"It's all right." His lips brushed her cheek, her temple, her hair. She was ice-cold and quivering. "You're all right."

Reaching out with his left hand, he pressed the template on the wall that turned on the overhead halozite light. The radiant bulb was on a sensor, and, not wanting to startle her further, he purposefully kept the setting low, making the room appear to have been lit by flickering candlelight.

Her face was as pale as the ice in Castle Mountain harbor back home, her eyes wide and unfocused. The pins holding her blond hair in its tidy coronet atop her head had fallen out during their brief struggle, and now her thick braid hung loose and limp over her shoulder. Her silky gown was drenched all the way through to the skin and her teeth were chattering.

"It was only a nightmare," he crooned, holding her terrified face between his palms. "You're safe, Julianna. Safe with me."

Still caught up in the horror of the nightmare, comprehension was not quick in coming. Her hands, which were pushing with all their might against his broad shoulders, gradually lowered. They were unfettered, Julianna realized vaguely; no leaden weights circled her wrists. Tentatively she moved her legs, finding them, too, unsecured.

She blinked—once, twice, then a third time—struggling to focus on the face swimming in front of her.

"You were having a bad dream." The deep, comforting, strangely familiar voice soothed her tangled nerves just as his stroking touch eased her lingering fears. "That's all it was, Juls. A bad dream."

She tried to talk but found that fear had struck her mute. All she could do was tremble like a leaf in a hurricane-force wind on Ontarian.

Her nipples, pebbled from her chill, pressed against the damp gown. At the provocative sight, Dylan felt a low, warning ache in his groin. Forcing it down, he drew her closer, his hand against the back of her hair, encouraging her to rest her head against his shoulder.

It was a strong, wide shoulder, a distinctly male shoulder. Slowly, as she drew in deep, ragged breaths, Julianna felt her terror begin to subside, gradually replaced by a lulling calm.

She still had no idea who this man was. She was only immensely grateful he'd been here when she needed him so desperately.

When she didn't offer any resistance, he shifted their positions slightly, so that she was half sitting, half lying on his lap. He was still talking to her in that low reassuring voice, in a language she vaguely recognized, but didn't have the strength to translate. But the meaning was all too obvious.

She was safe.

And then, incredibly, as his soothing lips lingered at her temple, the cold dark waters that had threatened to drown her became a warm and gentle sea. Lifting her arms around his neck, Julianna allowed herself to float on those gentle swells.

"You saved my life," she murmured, still caught on some vague level between dream and reality. "I was drowning. And you rescued me."

Her bottom was pressed enticingly against the front of his flight suit, causing his body to respond in a painfully physical way it had failed to do during Kala's expert seduction attempt.

His aching erection pressed against the damp silk, and when Julianna cuddled even closer, Dylan thought he'd ignite, the fire she created in him was so hot.

"It was only a dream," he repeated woodenly, reminding himself that she still wasn't coherent. To take advantage of a woman—any woman, but especially his best friend's sister—in this condition would be a crime. The idea was also terrifyingly tempting.

"You weren't drowning, Julianna." His voice was rough and unfamiliar to his own ears. "You're here on the *Mutiny*. With me."

"With you." She smiled sweetly and pressed her lips against his throat. Dylan bit back a groan and tried again.

"Juls." Although it took every ounce of self-restraint he possessed, he pulled her slender arms from around his neck and put her a little away from him, forcing her to look him directly in the face. "Do you even know who I am?"

He watched the soft pleasure on her face gradually fade, replaced by a vulnerability that tore at something deep inside him. Something frighteningly more elemental than mere sexual need.

"You're the man who saved me," she said on an unsteady whisper.

"Got it on the first try. Let's try for two."

She stared at him uncomprehendingly. "Two?"

"What's my name?"

"I don't remember." Her voice cracked with emotion, with all the fear she'd refused to let him see earlier.

"I'm Dylan. Dylan Prescott." Her hands had turned to ice again in his. He rubbed them briskly in an attempt to keep the blood flowing. "Starbuck's friend, remember?"

"Starbuck? My brother?" It all came crashing back like a tidal wave. "You're Dylan. From Earth. From another time."

Julianna closed her eyes, took a deep breath and let it out again. When she opened her eyes, she was too ashamed to look Dylan in the face. Instead, she directed her gaze over his right shoulder.

Dylan could tell she was struggling valiantly for control. He'd seen Starbuck make the same effort and had wondered what it must feel like to have his Sarnian and human sides constantly at war.

Starbuck had assured him that although Julianna was mindblind, in every other way she was a purely unemotional Sarnian. But as brilliant as Starbuck admittedly was, Dylan knew that in regard to his sister, he'd been way off the mark.

"I apologize for behaving like a frightened, hysterical female." Her voice was faint and tinged with self-reproach.

"While there's definitely no denying that you're a female, Juls, and a very attractive one at that, there's no need to apologize."

When she still refused to look at him, he took hold of her chin and gently turned her humiliated gaze his way. "About being hysterical, anyone can have a bad dream. Believe me, I've had my share.

"And as for being frightened, if you weren't a little scared right now, I'd be worried about your sanity."

She'd witnessed an amazing range of feelings from this man, which wasn't surprising, since terrans were well-known for their emotionalism. But Julianna couldn't help being impressed by the way, except for that one earlier display of temper, he continued to remain so unflinchingly calm in such a desperate situation.

"I suppose it would be only logical to be concerned about one's impending death," she decided reluctantly.

Dylan wanted to smile at her grave expression, but understanding how important logic was to a properly bred Sarnian, he didn't want her to think he was belittling her.

"Eminently logical," he agreed, managing, with effort, to match her formal tone.

He turned off the light, casting the room into shadows again. "But you're not going to die. At least not while I'm around. So, why don't we get you out of that wet dress. Then we can go back to sleep."

"I cannot take off my clothing. I have nothing else to put on," Julianna protested. Although it was dark, the idea of stripping naked in the same room with this man was impossible.

He picked, from the floor, the thin silver space blanket she'd kicked off during her nightmare and draped it over her, pulling it up to her chin.

"Now you're decent," he assured her. "If it'll make you feel better, I'll turn around, and you can slip the dress off beneath the blanket. It should be dry by morning."

It was, Julianna decided, a most logical solution. Holding the blanket against her with one hand, she managed to strip off the damp gown with the other. And then, after a moment's hesitation, the filmy chemise she was wearing underneath.

"I'm finished," she said softly.

The sound of her wiggling around beneath that blanket, and the thought of her nude body conspired to drive him crazy. What was it about Julianna Valderian that had him acting like an oversexed fourteen-year-old boy?

He took the wet clothing from her, noting that her hand was still uncomfortably cold. He draped the silky gown over a chair, followed by a filmy piece of feminine apparel so soft it could have been spun of milkweed. The material carried her scent.

Spreading the gossamer undergarment out beside her silvery gown, Dylan returned to the narrow bunk, testing his self-control by drawing her unprotestingly into his arms again.

"Go to sleep, Juls," he murmured against the top of her hair. "Then, in the morning we'll put our heads together and make plans to get the hell off this ship."

For some reason she would think about later, when her head was clearer, Julianna had not a single doubt that somehow Dylan Prescott would manage such an impossible feat. She also liked the idea that he believed her input would be helpful.

"In the morning," she agreed, her voice thickening.

The fear and tension had drained out of her. She was relaxed and warm and very delectable.

As she curled against him, like a kitten settling down for the night, her breath soft and slow against his neck, Dylan knew that Julianna would sleep now.

But he wouldn't.

6

THE NIGHT WAS AS LONG as a Maine winter. Longer.

Finally, frustrated and aching, Dylan untangled himself from Julianna's soft, warm body and dragged himself over to the absent captain's desk, where he spent the lonely hours until dawn working on an escape plan.

Much, much later, it was the *tap tap tap* of his fingers on the computer pad that woke her. Momentarily confused, Julianna looked around the unfamiliar surroundings. When her gaze focused on the dark-haired man seated at the desk, working intently at the computer, memory came crashing down on her.

She recalled the trial, Dylan Prescott's unexpected and for a time, unbelievable arrival, along with his during command of the prison transport ship.

She remembered the voluptuous, seductive Kala, and how he'd surprised her by sending the android prostitute away, and then, uncomfortably, she remembered the way her own rebellious body had responded to him in such an unsettling, human fashion.

And finally, she remembered the terrifying nightmare of drowning, and how she'd cried out in the night and how Dylan had once again come to her rescue, holding her, soothing her, yet in a strange and unfamiliar way, exciting her at the same time.

She remembered how wonderful she'd felt in his arms, how strong and comforting his body had felt against hers. She remembered the dark, mysterious male taste of his flesh as she'd pressed her mouth against his throat.

And then she remembered, with a sudden shock of Sarnian shame, taking off her clothing. Not just her dress but her chemise, as well!

But perhaps that embarrassing memory was merely part of her nightmare. Perhaps it hadn't really happened at all. Risking a peek beneath the thin silver blanket, she saw that she was, indeed, as nude as the day she'd entered the world from her mother's human womb.

Afraid that Dylan would think her no more discreet than Kala, Julianna was tempted to close her eyes, go back to sleep and try to hide from both her personal embarrassment and the unpalatable future looming ever nearer.

But, being a realist, and also curious as to what exactly Dylan was up to, she decided to get up and face whatever the Fates had planned for her today.

"Good morning," she said softly.

"Morning."

He'd discarded the orange flight suit sometime during the night and was clad only in a pair of white briefs. His broad chest was as dark and hard looking as the granitine cliffs on Australiana. His legs were long and well muscled. Julianna vaguely recalled those dark legs being entwined with hers sometime during the night.

If he was at all embarrassed by his state of undress, Dylan didn't reveal it. Engrossed in study, he didn't even bother to take his eyes from the flat amber computer screen. She recognized that ability to concentrate so intently—she'd often teased Starbuck that a meteor could strike and destroy the entire planet and if he were at work at the computer, he wouldn't even notice.

So much for being afraid that he'd try to take advantage of last night's vulnerability and seduce her, Julianna considered, wondering why she felt somewhat disappointed. Logically she should be grateful that his interest in her seemed to have waned.

Wrapping the blanket tightly around herself, she left the bunk and padded barefoot across the narrow room. She stood behind Dylan and looked over his shoulder.

"Is that a diagram of this ship?"

Dylan pressed a button, narrowing in on the schematic. "It's the engineering bay. I think I've just about got the place memorized."

"The entire ship?"

"Sarnians aren't the only ones with eidetic memories." His fingers stopped their dancing across the pad and he turned to look up at her. "That was one thing Starbuck and I discovered we had in common. Everything I've ever seen, or read, or learned or experienced is retained in my mind."

"Everything?" she asked tentatively, thinking of how she'd welcomed him into her bed last night. And how, if he'd been inclined, she would have allowed him to do far more than merely sleep beside her.

He nodded. "Everything."

They exchanged a long look. For the first time in her life, Julianna realized that a person could actually be technically mindblind and still know precisely what another was thinking.

And what Dylan was currently thinking was enough to make her blood start humming in her veins.

Her lips were so horribly dry. Julianna licked them with the tip of her tongue, then realized she'd made a dangerous mistake when a flame rose, fast and hot, in that dangerous male gaze.

She was staring at him as if she'd never seen a man's naked chest before. That idea had Dylan wondering exactly how experienced Julianna Valderian was.

Although he'd never wanted to broach the subject with Starbuck, considering the galactic traveler's interest in Charity, he'd wondered how men and women shared sexual desire on the faraway planet.

Last night Julianna had answered that question when she'd told him that sex on Sarnia was mental. Now that, he decided, remembering how warm and soft she'd felt in his arms, was one helluva waste.

The raw energy in his gaze threatened to melt her bone marrow. Julianna decided that her emotional survival depended on her returning their thoughts to Dylan's computer trespassing.

"How did you breach security?"

Dylan shrugged. "It was a snap." He didn't take his eyes from hers. "The good Captain Kirkian obviously isn't very computer literate. The average eight-year-old hacker could probably break into this system easier than winning at Super Mario Bros."

A soft haze was floating over her mind. Julianna tried to focus her gaze on his lips, to better understand his words, but memories of shared kisses only made things worse.

"Super Mario Bros.?"

The question came out on a halting whisper. Now Dylan was watching Julianna's lips. Seductive memories merged, then tangled.

"It's a computer game kids play. On Earth."

"Oh."

Her softly breathed word made Dylan forget all about kid's games. "Starbuck told me you were the most intelligent woman he'd ever known," Dylan said. "But he failed to tell me how beautiful you are."

"I'm not beautiful."

Certainly not as beautiful as all those genetically designed Sarnian women populating her planet, Julianna considered. Not to mention all those perfect androids created solely for sex. Like the overly voluptuous Kala.

"I thought properly brought up Sarnians never lied."

"We don't. Truth is reason," Julianna quoted automatically the catechism she'd grown up with. "Reason, truth."

"All else is illogical," Dylan finished up for her.

His slow, seductive smile started the flitterfly wings fluttering again in her stomach. Julianna lowered her eyes.

"Yes."

"Then know that I'm telling you the truth when I say that you are, without a doubt, the most beautiful woman I've ever seen."

"I am far from perfect," Julianna felt obliged to point out.

His judicious gaze skimmed her from head to toe. "You look pretty perfect to me."

Truth was deeply ingrained, all the way to the bone. "I have breasts."

Another smile, this one tinged with irony. "Don't remind me. I spent a long and painful night trying not to think about how perfectly they'd fit in my hand." The enticing smile reached his eyes, turning them the hue of gleaming cobalt.

"Do you have any idea how hard it was to concentrate on engineering schematics when I wanted to come back to that bunk with you and feel those soft womanly breasts pressed against my chest again?"

She could feel the unfamiliar flare of heat rising in her cheeks yet again at such a personal discussion. Having grown up in a society where flat-chested women were the ideal, she'd come to think of her rounded breasts, an inheritance from her human mother, as a fatal flaw she was forced to live with.

Indeed, more than one potential bondmate over the years had suggested that she have the cumbersome and unsightly orbs surgically removed.

"You are very frank."

"I try. Experience has taught me it's better to be upfront, particularly when dealing with women. Besides, knowing how you feel about honesty, I think it's best if I put all my cards on the table. I want to make love to you, Juls."

This time his gaze moved over her more slowly, caressing her face, her throat, pausing for a heart-stopping time at those breasts that had always been the bane of her existence, traveling downward, his pupils darkening as they lingered at that suddenly hot, damp place between her legs. Desire rose in her like a sirocco, causing her thighs to quake.

"Making love," she said, schooling her voice to the properly stiff tone she would have used to read a paper on terran behavior at an intergalactic xenoanthropological convention. "Is that a terran colloquial term for physical sexual congress?"

Now that he'd discovered Julianna's heat, Dylan was finding it rather enjoyable when she pulled out that ice maiden routine. The contrast was undeniably appealing.

"I suppose you could put it that way. But believe me, Juls, it's a helluva lot more fun than you make it sound."

He surprised her by grabbing hold of her hips and pulling her down onto his lap. Later, Julianna knew she would berate herself for not resisting. But at the moment, it felt so good, so right, to be in his arms again.

He took her hand, lifted it and kissed each finger, one at a time, before pressing them against his bare chest.

"Feel that?"

An arrowing of ebony hair disappeared beneath the elastic waistband of his briefs. She was surprised to find that the curls were silky, not crisp and rough as they appeared. As her fingers toyed in the jet curls, his heartbeat, which was strong and sure, increased dramatically. As did hers.

"That's what you do to me, Juls. That, among other more uncomfortable things."

The increased rate of his pulse, the feel of his sex burgeoning beneath her, imbued Julianna with a sense of feminine power like nothing she'd ever known.

"Are you complaining?"

The coy tone was exactly the same one that had been programmed in Kala. If she weren't feeling so dizzy, if her blood weren't beating so loudly in her ears, and if she weren't so suddenly, desperately needy, Julianna would have been shocked to hear it coming from between her own lips.

"Not really." Dylan leaned his head against the back of the captain's chair and closed his eyes as her exploring fingers, working on instinct alone, inched their way down his bare flesh like feathery brands.

When they began to slip beneath the waistband of the soft cotton briefs, he sucked in a deep breath. This was insane, he reminded himself. He had enough problems right now without complicating matters by sleeping with a woman who was obviously still a virgin. A woman who was also his soon-to-be-brother-in-law's younger sister.

He curled his fingers around her wrist, forestalling her erotic caress.

"You'd better get dressed. Before I forget that I'm a gentleman. And your brother's best friend."

His brusque tone hurt her more than a physical slap against her flaming cheek. Humiliated and inexplicably furious by his abrupt rejection, Julianna quickly stood up.

"I'm going to take a shower first," she said, tugging the blanket even tighter around her throbbing body as she glared down at him. "When I return, I would appreciate you having put your own clothing on. Being human is no excuse to run around barely clad, like some oversexed, barbarian pirate."

She scooped up her now-dry clothing and was gone, entering the adjoining room, which held a narrow sonic shower stall. Seconds later, giving in to the unruly temper this man seemed able to ignite so easily in her, Julianna slammed the door behind her.

Dylan stared at the closed door for a long, thoughtful moment. He sighed.

Then, reminding himself that the task at hand was to keep the surprisingly passionate, distractingly tempting Julianna Valderian alive, Dylan returned his attention to the ever-changing graphics on Captain Kirkian's computer screen.

Julianna stood in the sonic shower stall, arms outstretched, head thrown back, eyes closed as her body was quickly and efficiently cleansed.

She grimaced with lingering mortification, wishing that her mind could be so easily cleansed of the seductive images that were flashing through her mind like scenes from an old-fashioned laser disk. . . . Dylan lifting her down from the shuttlecraft, his touch creating a disconcerting flare of heat at her waist. The shocking, thrilling kiss they'd shared on the bridge, and later, the pleasurable, strangely comforting feeling of lying in his arms as he soothed her nightmare away with words and gentle hands.

Julianna wanted to forget the way this strange, unpredictable man from the faraway world and distant time could make her ache; she didn't want to recall the tactile pleasure she'd received from touching his chest, and she certainly wished that she could stop wondering what it would feel like to have him touch her in that same way.

With her eyes still closed tightly, she cupped her breasts in her palms, imagining her hands were Dylan's hands. When her unruly mind conjured up the image of his dark thumbs brushing against her nipples in precisely the way she was currently doing, guilt flooded through her, along with a pleasure she suspected was totally forbidden by proper Sarnian society. A soft, ragged sigh slipped from between her parted lips.

Caught up in the first sexual fantasy of her life, Julianna plucked at her nipples, now pebbled as hard as stones, and felt a corresponding tug between her thighs. She could feel herself becoming moist again down there in that secret, forbidden place, and longed to touch that tingling flesh as well.

But her deep-seated Sarnian restraint kept her hands where they were. On her full and aching human breasts. Such alien sensual pleasure was enough, for now.

And even as she gave herself permission to enjoy it for what it was—a purely scientific sexual experiment—Julianna feared that soon, very soon, she would be wanting more.

Her next thought, as she reluctantly returned her mind to reality and proceeded to dress, was that for the human side of her mind, at least, there was a very fine line between want and need. The challenge would be not to cross it.

WHAT THE HELL was she doing in there? Dylan gave up trying to work. He wished that he could tell himself that his uncharacteristic response to Julianna Valderian was because he'd been so wrapped up in his work, because he'd been without a woman too long. But technically that wasn't true.

Oh, it had been nearly a month since he'd been with Vanessa Reynolds, the woman he'd mistakenly allowed to share his Maine laboratory—and his bed—only to discover, when she and her henchmen nearly killed him and kidnapped Starbuck, that she'd made love with him simply in order to steal his quantum jump data.

But, although he'd always enjoyed women, and certainly enjoyed the myriad pleasures of the bedroom, four weeks of forced celibacy wasn't all that unusual. Not when he was engrossed in his work.

So, since he couldn't blame his current inability to concentrate on sexual abstinence, he'd simply have to discover some other logical reason.

While Dylan would never claim to adhere to that strict, unwavering logic that Sarnian citizens were taught to strive for, a lifetime of scientific experimentation had taught him that there was always an understandable reason for every phenomenon. Now all he had to do was figure out what it was.

Which he'd do. As soon as he could stop thinking about taking Julianna's lush breast into his mouth.

As SHE'D INSTRUCTED, he'd dressed while she'd been showering. But instead of the orange flight suit he'd worn the previous day, now he was clad in a black shirt and black pants tucked into a pair of high, gleaming black boots. The clothing belonged to the absent Captain Kirkian, Julianna decided.

The black garments made him look more the rogue pirate she'd first thought him to be. They also made him appear, she admitted reluctantly, even more dashing.

As she moved toward him, her gossamer gown shifted, reminding Dylan of the soft body beneath it. She was so lovely he almost forgot what he'd been planning to say.

"I think I've figured out a plan." He was grateful when his voice sounded remarkably normal.

"Oh?" The sensual warmth he thought he saw in her amber eyes immediately vanished, replaced by curiosity. "To escape?"

"Yep." He turned toward the computer. "Give me the shuttlecraft bay."

"Scanning," the feminine voice agreed instantly. It was, Julianna noted, the same seductive voice that had been programmed into Kala. Obviously, Captain Kirkian had preferred his females to purr like sleek pussycats.

She stood behind Dylan's shoulder, watching as the computer scanned backward through the schematics before finally coming to a stop.

"Here is the shuttlecraft bay, Captain," the voluptuous voice offered.

"Terrific. How about a close-up of one of the pods?" Dylan requested.

"Whatever you say, Captain."

The screen narrowed in on a small two-man pod. Dylan glanced up at Julianna. "I don't suppose you know how to pilot one of those."

"No."

"No problem," he assured her. "We'll figure it out. It can't be all that much harder than learning to drive a stick shift."

Julianna drew in a quick breath as she realized what he was thinking. "Won't the crew be suspicious if you suddenly decide to abandon ship? With your prisoner?"

He lifted a shoulder in a negligent shrug. "They won't know. There's only one guard in the bay. As for the rest of the crew, we can create a small emergency that'll hold their attention long enough to get away from here."

The idea was ridiculously dangerous. It was also undeniably exciting.

"But when they do discover we're missing, won't they begin to search for us?"

"They might," Dylan agreed. "But I figure that even though technology and space exploration has made the star systems smaller, a person can still get lost if he wants to. After all, you're the one who told me about transport pilots being expert smugglers."

"True, but, in case you've forgotten, you're not actually a transport pilot."

"Don't worry about a thing, Juls," Dylan said with that same cocky self-confidence that Julianna suspected would sound like insufferable ego on a lesser man. "We're going to make it off this ship safe and sound."

"And then what?" She wondered what he'd say when she informed him that she intended to return to Sarnia, and suspected that he would not be all that enthusiastic about the idea.

He grinned up at her. "Let's just take this one step at a time, okay?"

Such step-by-step behavior was, Julianna considered, eminently logical. So why didn't she feel more confident? She was about to question him further, when he turned around and began tapping again on the computer keypad.

"Are you certain this is what you want me to do, Captain?"

"Absolutely."

"But cryogenics is only used on flights to far-off systems," the computer argued. "On sleeper ships when the journey encompasses several light-years."

Dylan was not accustomed to having a machine argue with him. "I'm well aware of the study of cryogenics, computer," he said sharply, wondering yet again at the technique that had been employed to teach these man-made computers artificial intelligence. "But I wish to reprogram the ship's cooling system nevertheless."

There was a moment's silence. Dylan wondered if the female computer was actually sulking. "Yes, sir," the feminine voice said finally.

Dylan patted the top of the amber monitor. "That's my girl."

Then he turned to Julianna. "We'd better go ahead and eat breakfast before we take off. I'll fill you in on the specifics while we choke down another serving of UFO."

"UFO?" Julianna recalled from ancient history disks that terrans had used such an acronym for unidentified flying objects.

"Unidentified food object," Dylan translated.

Intrigued in spite of herself at what he had in mind, Julianna nodded her agreement.

Then, as if on cue, the cyborg Dylan had pressed into service the previous night arrived with two covered plates on a metal tray. The breakfast was, unsurprisingly, as unappealing and as unrecognizable as last night's dinner. Dylan found himself fantasizing about a tall stack of golden pancakes drowning in sweet maple syrup, thick slices of Canadian bacon, two eggs—cooked over easy—and some biscuits on the side.

Thirty minutes later, they were making their way through the maze of narrow hallways again. Doors obediently opened, as if by unseen servants, then slid silently closed behind them.

"Remember what you're supposed to do?" Dylan asked as they approached the air lock to the pod bay.

Julianna nodded. "I remember. But I am not certain that I am capable of such subterfuge."

"Don't worry about a thing. There isn't a red-blooded male anywhere in any universe who wouldn't find you a distraction."

She never would have considered being a distraction a positive attribute, yet the warmth in Dylan's tone suggested he'd meant the unflattering term as a compliment. Realizing that the terran mind—at least the mind of this particular terran—was far more complex than she'd been taught to believe, Julianna decided not to dwell on things she could not understand.

"The computer revealed that the guard in the pod bay is Janurian," she reminded him.

"So?"

"So Janurian blood is green, not red."

"Whatever. Just look at him the way you were look-ing at me when you came out of the shower this morn-ing and the guy's a goner."

If he was truly a gentleman, as he'd claimed, Ju-lianna thought, he wouldn't have mentioned her mor-tifying lapse in self-restraint.

"I was not looking at you in any way."

"You know, Juls," he said easily, "if you insist on be-ing a true Sarnian, you're going to have to do some-thing about this unfortunate tendency of yours to lie."

She opened her mouth to argue, but they'd reached the air lock leading to the pod bay.

Dylan stopped just long enough to frame her face between his palms. His intelligent blue eyes moved slowly, judiciously, over her in much the same way they had when he'd first materialized at her home.

"Although I wish I'd thought to tell you to get rid of that Swedish librarian's braid, you still look abso-lutely gorgeous this morning," he said. "But some-thing's missing."

His thoughtful gaze roved her face, creating warmth wherever it touched, finally settling on her lips. "Aha. Got it," he murmured, more to himself than to her.

And then, at the exact same moment Julianna read Dylan's intention in his midnight-blue eyes, his dark head swooped down and he kissed her again.

Hard.

7

DYLAN ENDED THE KISS long before Julianna was ready for him to.

Her head was still spinning as he gave her another quick study and said, "Perfect." His broad grin was cocky and entirely too self-satisfied. "Let's get this show on the road, sweetheart."

Julianna felt a surge of fury that he took his sexual power for granted. But having always prided herself on her intelligence, she knew this was not the time to get into a long, drawn out argument.

So, deciding to save her blistering verbal assault for after they'd escaped the prison ship, Julianna took a deep breath and concentrated on returning her drumming heartbeat to something close to normal.

That goal achieved, she ran through a mental imaging of her next move. She was, Dylan had told her, the key to their escape. And then he'd blithely proceeded to give her the most difficult assignment of her life.

What if she couldn't do it?

"Julianna."

Dylan's deep voice, so calm and gentle, without a hint of his usual teasing, drew her tentative gaze up to his.

"You'll be fine." He ran the back of his hand down her cheek. Unspoken concern faded from her worried eyes, replaced by the soft yearning he was beginning to find so appealing. "Better than fine. You'll be downright spectacular."

With that encouragement ringing in her ears, Julianna took another deep breath, then entered the air lock on the sultry, hip-swiveling glide she'd copied from Kala.

The guard, surprised by her sudden appearance, failed to notice Dylan slip into the shuttlecraft bay behind her. As the air lock shut, the computer in the captain's quarters began, as programmed, to lower the temperature in the rest of the ship.

Every atom of his body on red alert, Dylan stood in the shadows and watched as Julianna went into her act.

Less than a minute had passed when something that Dylan uncomfortably recognized as jealousy curled through his gut.

It had been a carefully thought-out, albeit risky, strategy. His instructions had been specific. To charm the Janurian guard long enough for Dylan to take him out.

But he didn't recall telling her to stand so damn close. Hell, her thighs were practically touching his. And although he'd been the one to put it there in the first place, Dylan was infuriated by the gleam that turned her eyes to burnished gold and promised pleasures a man would die for.

And he knew damn well he hadn't told her to press those slender white fingers against the man's broad chest.

In answer to the guard's question as to what Ju- Julianna was doing in the shuttlecraft bay, she pretended tears, begging him to protect her from the *Mutiny*'s brutal captain.

And then, using feminine wiles she hadn't even known she possessed two days ago, she was supposed to let the guard believe that his payment for such sanctuary would definitely be worth the risk.

It was, Dylan admitted, going precisely according to plan, therefore, why was he so angry? Because, he answered, Julianna's performance was turning out to be far better than he ever would have predicted.

He watched the slow, tantalizing smile curve her lips, lips Dylan could taste even now. His fingers clenched into tight fists as her hand crept up the guard's massive chest and brushed along his bearded, now slack, jaw. He ground his teeth as she went up on her toes, her smiling mouth headed straight toward the Janurian's lips.

Just as the guard's eyes glazed over, Dylan stepped out of the shadows and delivered a fast, hard left punch to his jaw. Two semesters of boxing in college had trained him well. The Janurian didn't know what hit him. He crumpled to the floor, his black eyes rolled back in their sockets.

Standing over him, Dylan flexed his aching fingers.

"You actually enjoyed that," Julianna gasped, view- ing the expression of satisfaction on his face. Physical violence was abhorrent to her. As it was to all properly brought-up Sarnians.

"Probably about as much as you enjoyed watching that Neanderthal fall under the spell of your seduction tactics," he accused, glowering down at her.

She stared up at him, surprise warring with anger. Anger won out. "I was only following your instructions," she spat back.

He snorted scoffingly. "I sure as hell don't remember telling you to have so much fun."

At that, Julianna muttered something so un-Sarnian, so unladylike, Dylan's jealousy disintegrated. He laughed. At himself, at her, at this unbelievable situation.

"When we have more time," he told her, his tone returning to its normal easy one, "I'll teach you the fun of making up after an argument."

He shot a quick glance at the unconscious guard. "But right now, I think we ought to get out of here."

With unspoken agreement, she clambered into the passenger seat of the compact two-man pod.

She was not surprised when it only took him moments to figure out the computer controls. Although it had taken her a while to believe his seemingly outrageous statement that he was, indeed, Dylan Prescott, she now knew that she was in the presence of one of the most brilliant men of all time.

What all those history books and journals had failed to state, Julianna considered, as the pod shot out of the shuttle bay like a little slingshot from gravity into the endless, star-pierced darkness, was exactly how masculine, how seductive, the man was.

She wished she'd paid more attention to whatever biographical information had been written about the terran scientist. There was so much she suddenly wanted to know. First and foremost, was he married?

The idea of Dylan bonded with some other woman was so unpalatable Julianna refused to dwell on it.

Unable to resist, she looked behind her. From this viewpoint, the *Mutiny* appeared massive. With the running lights gleaming in the darkness, Julianna could read the letters spelling out the ship's name, number, planet of registry.

"Everyone on board should be out cold," Dylan said. "By the time they wake up and realize we're gone, we'll be far out of sensor range."

His plan to drop the temperature of the ship to below freezing, using cryogenics to put the crew into a deep, long-voyage sleep, was, Julianna admitted, quite clever. As was his resetting the ship's course, sending it out into the far reaches of the galaxy, out of communication range with both Sarnia and Australiana.

"But when I fail to arrive, won't the Australianan officials notify the Ruling Council?" She asked the question that had been nagging at her since he'd first revealed his plan.

"Probably."

"So? What we will do?"

He shot her a quick, sideways glance and gave her another one of those cocky, all-too-human grins. "We punt."

She had no idea what he was talking about. But just when she was about to argue, she recalled an ancient terran saying of her mother's about not borrowing trouble.

Deciding that there was some merit to that old adage, Julianna let Dylan's unfamiliar remark pass without comment.

To Dylan's surprise, they were seated in front of real windows, not some computer viewscreen. As the pod raced through the silent, star-studded darkness, he felt as if he were sitting at the twenty-second-century equivalent of a ship's prow.

The fact that he had scant idea where they were headed made him empathize with those long-ago daring explorers who'd headed out onto unknown seas, seeking new worlds.

Although things were certainly not turning out at all as he and Starbuck had planned, Dylan had to admit that he was finding this adventure far more stimulating than his customary scientific study. In fact, he was having one helluva good time.

"This is great," he murmured. "I feel like a twenty-second-century Indiana Jones."

"Indiana Jones?"

Before he could explain the pod began to rock violently.

"It's a meteor shower," Julianna said, flinching as one the space rocks flew by the window.

"Damn." Dylan struggled gamely with the controls, cursing as they were buffeted from all directions. "Hold on."

He needn't have bothered with that instruction. Julianna was clutching the edge of her seat so tightly her knuckles were white.

He could do it, she kept telling herself over and over, like a mantra. *Dylan will keep us safe.*

The ship rocked violently as the storm grew worse. Then there was an enormous jolt that, in spite of her seat belt, nearly flung her from the chair.

Dylan ground out a particularly virulent curse. "We've been hit," he muttered, punching up the damage on the dashboard computer monitor. The collision had set off the harsh, strident Klaxon sound of an onboard warning system.

"Damage in the rear quadrant," a calm female voice reported.

"We're going to have to land this baby."

"Land?" Smoke began to fill the compact compartment. Julianna coughed as she stared out into the unending darkness. "Where?"

He punched a few more buttons, revealing a close-up map of their sector of the galaxy. "We're in luck. There's an asteroid just below us."

She groaned inwardly as she recognized exactly where they were. The barren rock was reputedly home to space pirates, renegade Janurian warriors, disreputable transport pilots and other space riffraff.

"That's Number 229. We can't land there. It's too dangerous."

The pod was beginning to spin out of control. Dylan wrestled with the guidance system. "Why not? Won't the place support human life?"

The siren blared. The voice of the computer reported additional damage, plus a fire in the mechanical system, and recommended all parties abandon ship.

"It will, but—"

Another, smaller piece of hurling rock struck the windshield, creating a starburst effect in the thick quartzalite pane. "Then that's where we're going."

He certainly seemed calm enough, considering the circumstances, Julianna thought, watching as he tapped the course correction into the computer.

"Now cross your fingers," he said on a voice so mild they could have been discussing the weather.

Correction entered, the blinking screen reported. An instant later the voice confirmed the change in course.

Dylan smiled grimly, reminding himself that he'd always been lucky. "Okay. Here we go. Hang on tight, Juls. And put your head down on your knees." A crack ripped across the instrument panel. Orange flames began licking from the narrow fissure. "I have a feeling this isn't going to be a textbook three-point landing."

Fear shimmered down her spine. Doing as instructed, Julianna lowered her head to her knees, then closed her eyes. And then, although the ancient gods, long ago declared illogical, had been removed from all Sarnian calendars, she prayed.

Gravity pulled the pod downward, air friction made its surface burn. As the ground began to rush up at them, a jagged chunk of metal tore off the two-person ship, spiraling out into space. And then another.

Bolts began to tear loose, flying around the compartment like bullets from a machine gun. Dylan kept his eyes on the horizon and prayed he could land the crumbling ship before it disintegrated completely.

Once again luck proved to be with him as they landed, with a jolt, nose first.

"Welcome to asteroid Number 229," Dylan said, as the pod came to a shuddering halt into an enormous red sand dune. "And thank you for flying Air Prescott."

Unfortunately, their troubles were far from over. Outside the damaged pod, a storm raged, driving blood red sand against the cracked windshield.

Hurricane-force winds blew the red grains through the many fissures in the pod, stinging their skin like shards of broken glass, burning the eyes.

The storm continued for hours. Unable to do anything else, Dylan and Julianna clung to each other, heads bent, eyes closed tight, as the wind wailed and the red sand flogged at them like harsh whips.

Even worse than the wind and sand, Julianna discovered, was the fear that had tightened like a fist around her heart. Although she knew such an idea was fanciful, she saw death hovering on her shoulder, like a patient black carrion-eating bird.

Finally blessed silence fell over the ship. The wind had stopped. The storm had passed.

"Thank God," Dylan breathed, lifting his head and looking around. Everything on board the pod, he and Julianna included, was coated with a covering of red silt. "There was a minute there, I thought I heard the elephant."

Julianna lifted exhausted, red-rimmed eyes. "There are no elephants on 229."

Feeling remarkably better, he bent his head and brushed his grimy lips against hers. "It's a saying pioneers used to have out on the Great Plains. When the wind blew for days and days without a respite, people sometimes went crazy."

Julianna could certainly identify with that. During the horrid storm, the wind screeching in her ears had begun to sound like lost, alien souls.

"I heard it, too," she admitted.

"But we made it, Juls. Safe and sound."

For now. At the thought of what type of unsavory inhabitants were undoubtedly waiting to pounce on them outside the pod, Julianna trembled.

Mistaking the reason for her shivers, believing them to be a lingering reaction to the storm, Dylan squeezed her shoulder comfortingly.

"Let's see if the computer's still working. We can use it to find the nearest town."

It was, just barely. Although the female voice of the computer had been silenced, the graphics system still functioned. If the data displayed on the screen was accurate, the nearest settlement appeared to be within walking distance.

But as she started out across the barren red landscape with Dylan, Julianna's heart was filled with dread. She was beginning to wish she'd taken her chances on the prison ship.

The dunes went on forever, vast, red, rolling away to the horizon. Heat-buoyed dust devils skittered across the landscape, lifting sand upward in small funnel clouds.

A huge yellow sun, resembling the one on Earth, but much, much hotter, blazed overhead in a cloudless blue sky, heating the ground and blistering the skin.

After more than two hours of trudging through the immense red range, Dylan was beginning to regret his decision. He was hot, sweaty, and beginning to worry that he and Julianna would die of dehydration before they ever reached civilization.

As they finally made their way to the crest of one particularly high dune, he stopped in his tracks.

"That's gotta be a mirage," he said, squinting at the sparkling aquamarine pool surrounded by palm trees. The enticing scene could have come directly from the glossy cover of a Caribbean travel brochure.

"Or a hallucination." Perhaps, Dylan considered grimly, he was suffering from a severe case of heatstroke.

"It's an oasis," Julianna assured him. "Nomadic tribesmen water their beasts of burden at such watering holes."

"And wash off the sand, too, I bet." Dylan felt as if he were carrying an extra ten pounds of the gritty red stuff on his aching hot body. "Is the water safe?"

"Oh, yes," Julianna said. "The water is one of the few things that is safe on 229."

Dylan ignored the veiled warning. "Terrific. Let's go."

He crossed his arms over his chest, pulled up the hem of the captain's black shirt and pulled it over his head. He'd sat down on the sand and was unlacing his boots when he realized that Julianna hadn't moved.

"Something wrong?"

Her unwilling gaze was drawn to his bare chest. The slanting golden rays of the sun made the arrowing of hair on his chest gleam like jet. "Are you suggesting we bathe?"

"That's precisely what I'm suggesting." He yanked off first one boot, then the other. "Unless you like carrying around half an asteroid. No offense, Juls, but you look as if someone's dunked you headfirst into an enormous bin of red chili powder."

Although she had no idea what chili powder was, Julianna inferred from his tone that his words were not meant as a compliment.

"A bath sounds perfect." When his hands moved to the fastener of his trousers, Julianna turned her back. "Since you saved my life, it is only right that you go first. Let me know when you're finished."

He pulled the tight black pants down his legs and stepped out of them, leaving them abandoned on the sand. "You don't have to wait." His cotton briefs were no longer white; they'd been dyed pink by the sand that had filtered into his clothes during the violent storm.

An image of Dylan naked invaded Julianna's mind. She closed her eyes, tight. But the vision refused to fade. "I think it would be for the best."

"Don't tell me that you're afraid? After all we've already been through."

When she didn't answer, Dylan sighed. She was, he reminded himself, a woman of two worlds, torn between her reserved, logical Sarnian side and her more emotional, intuitive human side.

"How about we make a deal?"

"A deal?"

She glanced back over her shoulder, then wished she hadn't. It was the first time in all her twenty-five years of existence that she'd seen a naked male.

Entranced in spite of herself, she wondered if all human men were so magnificently formed. And then, even more dangerously, she wondered how that hard masculine body would feel pressed against her own naked one, thighs to thighs, belly to belly, chest to chest. She turned away, closed her eyes again and pressed her lips together. Hard.

"A bargain," he translated. "A sort of compromise."

Dylan was glad she'd turned her back to him again. The shock of desire he'd seen flash across her dusty red face had made him hard. Again. It seemed as if Starbuck's sister was destined to keep him in a constant state of arousal.

"What type of bargain?" she asked numbly.

Her mouth, already dry, had turned as arid as the barren landscape. She tried to make herself believe that it was the blazing sun overhead that had her feeling so hot. She failed.

"I'll go ahead and get in, then turn my back while you undress. Once you're in the water, I won't be able to see a thing you don't want me to."

It was an eminently logical solution. And she was so hot and so tired of the sand sticking like glue to her sweaty skin.

"All right. That is an acceptable compromise."

Dylan entered the pool on a sharp dive, slicing through the cool water that shocked his skin on first contact, then blissfully soothed.

"Come on in, Juls," he called out to her. "The water's great."

She discarded her own clothes, then made her way to the water's edge. As promised, he'd turned his back, although it wasn't much help to her ragged composure. Because Julianna found the sight of that dark flesh stretched over supple muscles nearly as unsettling as his chest.

Instead of diving right in as Dylan had done, Julianna waded cautiously into the pool, enjoying the cooling feel of the water first against her feet, then her calves, then her thighs.

When the blue water reached her waist, she closed her eyes and sank the rest of the way beneath the surface.

It was, in a word, sublime.

When she surfaced, she found Dylan treading water only inches away.

"Feeling better?" he asked, shaking back his wet hair.

"Vastly." The water was clear enough that she could see his chest. Seeking control, she tried to concentrate her attention on his face. It didn't help. A devil she was beginning to recognize gleamed wickedly in his dark eyes.

The sandy bottom was beyond her toes. Julianna kicked to keep herself afloat.

The water lapped at her breasts. Dylan's hands practically itched with the need to touch them. Instead, utilizing a self-control he hadn't been aware of possessing, he forced them to keep making small figure eights just below the surface.

"You know, you're turning out to be a pretty good sport, Juls."

"You sound surprised."

"I suppose I am. You look so delicate, so ethereal, I didn't figure you'd turn out to have so much of what my Grandmother Prescott would have called good old-fashioned spunk."

"Spunk." She repeated the unfamiliar word aloud, liking the sound of it. "Does your sister have spunk?"

Dylan grinned. "Loads. I think that's one of the reasons Starbuck fell in love with her."

"Starbuck never believed in love," Julianna mused out loud.

"Well, he's definitely a believer now." With the subtlest movement of hands and legs, Dylan moved a little closer. "How about you?"

"Me?"

"What do you believe?"

Truth was reason. Reason, truth. "That the term is merely an outdated euphemism for biological desire," she parroted the Sarnian party line.

"I see." Deliberately he tangled his legs with hers at the same time his arms encircled Julianna, pulling her hard against him. "Speaking of biological desire..."

8

JUST AS IN HER EARLIER fantasy, his chest was taut against her breasts and she could feel his hard male sex pressing against her belly. The sexual charge between them was so strong Julianna was amazed that they hadn't set the water to boiling around them.

Her arms were trapped between their bodies, her legs caught between his. But Julianna didn't feel the slightest fear. Nor did she have any desire to move.

"I want to make love to you, Juls." His hands moved down her back, cupping her hips, lifting her so that she could feel the extent of his need.

"I, too, want that." She could no more deny the overwhelming truth than she could suddenly beam herself across the sparkling pool by astro-projection, the way her brother could have once done so effortlessly. "But first, there is something I must tell you."

Dylan was nibbling on her earlobe. "What's that?" he asked distractedly.

"Although intellectually I knew that I was not destined to live for very long after the trial, for some reason, which I suspect was due to an unfortunate human trait of denial, the enormity of my situation had not totally sunk in."

"Makes sense to me."

She was so sweet. So soft. So delectable. Thinking ahead of all the erotic things he was going to do with her, Dylan was only half-listening.

When he bit her neck, she felt a tingling rush of pleasure between her thighs. It was becoming more and more difficult to concentrate, but Julianna felt a very strong need to explain. It seemed immensely important that he understand the reason behind her uncharacteristic behavior.

Reason was truth. Truth, reason. All else was illogical.

"But then, during the sandstorm, I realized exactly how close I'd actually come to dying. And despite all that I had been taught about dying being nothing more than ceasing to exist, I was frightened."

He'd never met a woman quite like Julianna. She was brave and innocent, all at the same time. His tongue traced the inner convolutions of her ear. "I won't let anything happen to you, Juls. That's a promise."

"I know you will try to protect me." When one hand slid into the silky furrow of her bottom, Julianna's voice cracked. "But we still have a lot of dangers ahead."

"I'll handle them." His fingers continued their erotic quest, discovering the exquisitely tender flesh of her vaginal lips. His mouth plucked at hers as his fingers continued to torment her beneath the rippling surface of the water.

"We'll handle them together," he said, punctuating each word with a soft, tantalizing kiss.

His lips, his hands, were conspiring to make her lose her train of thought. Julianna's mind struggled against his sexual mastery even as her body willingly surrendered.

"But no one can predict the future," she argued on a soft moan of hunger. "Which is why I have decided to allow my human side to experience sexual relations once before I die."

She'd finally managed to garner his full attention. Dylan pulled his head back to look at her. Her remarkable eyes were so frank, her tone so matter-of-fact, that he couldn't decide which he wanted to do more—shake her senseless, or take her up on her less than romantic offer.

"You make it sound as if you're discussing the two of us taking part in some xenoanthropological experiment."

"That's precisely correct." Once again Julianna was both surprised and relieved that Dylan understood her meaning so quickly.

But she quickly discovered that Dylan was far from pleased. His curse was short, hard and blunt. "Are you always this damn logical?"

What was he so angry about? She'd told him the truth. And she was willing to have physical sex with him. So why was he suddenly looking at her as if he'd love to drown her?

"Of course. At least I attempt to be," she added, honesty requiring her to admit that she was not always successful in her quest for absolute rationality.

"Logic is a taught way of life, one that affects every Sarnian more profoundly than others, just as one religion or philosophy will affect a given earth person more than another," she explained, her voice instinctively slipping into her lecture tone.

"I have, of course, in my work, studied the physical details of sexual congress between terrans. However, since your arrival on Sarnia, I've been experiencing such new and unsettling feelings that I have decided that it would be only logical to engage in such human behavior, as an experiment."

Her analytical tone should have thrown icy water on any hunger he might have been feeling. But instead, it made Dylan want to drag her out of the sparkling blue pool, throw her down on the hot red sand beneath one of those palm trees and show her exactly what true passion felt like.

Then let her try for her damn logic when every atom in her body was poised on the brink of orgasm.

"For your information, Julianna, when I do take you to bed, we'll be making love, not having sexual congress for some stupid, anthropological inquiry."

He pulled her close again, rubbing his tumescent sex against her, letting her feel his raw masculine hunger. "And it damn well won't be a one-time thing, because I plan to make love to you all day and all night long, again and again, touching you everywhere, tasting every delectable bit of your sweet moist flesh.

"Then, when you're on fire, and you don't think you can stand it another minute, I'll fill you so fully, so tightly, so perfectly, that you'll finally submit your entire mind and body to me. Only me. And believe me, sweetheart, there won't be a damn logical thing about it."

His words affected her in the same way as his wicked, unruly hands, roaming her flesh beneath the water, were making her ache. Making her want.

Still, even through the assault he was creating on her senses, some lingering vestige of pride made itself known.

"I thought you were exceptional. Which was why I was willing to have sex with you. But you're not any different from the rogue terran transport pilot you pretended to be," she accused. "You only want a submissive, acquiescent female for your own lusty pleasures."

If he was at all wounded by her harsh condemnation, Dylan didn't reveal it. "Now that's where you're wrong, Juls." As he brushed his lips teasingly against hers, Julianna could feel his smile. "I'm all for women's equality. In the bedroom as well as in the boardroom . . . especially in the bedroom.

"Because while I'm driving you to the very brink, you're going to be doing the same thing to me, taking me deep inside you, embracing me all around with your womanly heat, hotter and hotter, until our flesh melts into one."

He slipped one finger high up inside her tight sheath, creating a flame that made her burn from the inside out.

"I don't understand." Her body clutched at him. Wanting, needing, more. "If you truly wish to have sexual relations with me, why did you become so angry when I offered myself to you?"

"I'm not really angry." Another finger slid into her moist warmth. "Just frustrated. Because you're going about this seduction thing all wrong, Juls."

"Then teach me the right way. I have always been a very quick learner," she assured him. "In fact, I finished first in my class at the Science Institute."

Damn it, the woman still didn't get it.

"I'm not one of your stupid laboratory rats," he said, biting off each word. "When I do make love to you, Julianna, it's going to be because you want it as badly as I do. When you're so hot and bothered, you're willing to beg me to take you."

"Beg?" She hadn't even begged for her life. How could this insufferable man think she would sink so low as to beg for something that was undoubtedly highly overrated?

Julianna tossed her head. Despite her mixed blood, her haughty manner was every bit that of a daughter fathered by a descendant of the Ancient Ones. The closest thing Sarnia had to royalty.

"I will never beg."

"Then I guess you'll never know true passion," he said mildly. "Or experience the absolute ecstasy when two people—male and female—become one."

Her lips had pulled into a tight, mutinous line. He pressed a kiss against them. Next, surprising her with an unexpected show of tenderness, he kissed the tip of her nose.

And then, without warning, he sank beneath the water, pulling her with him.

The water swirled around them, over them, as he captured her lips. His tongue probed and explored, tasting of her inner sweetness. Forgetting where and who she was, forgetting that she was furious at him again, Julianna returned the kiss eagerly, wrapping her legs around Dylan's waist, pressing her pelvis against him.

The kiss, which later she would realize had only lasted moments, seemed to go on for an eternity. Finally, when the air was gone from their lungs, they rose together, breaking the surface of the water.

"You'll beg," Dylan predicted with a masculine self-confidence she found maddening.

Julianna jerked free of his light hold, sputtering furiously. "I'll see you on your knees first," she shot back.

Dylan surprised her once again, laughing as she swam with furious, strong strokes toward the edge of the pool. "As a fellow scientist, I have a question for you."

She was getting accustomed to the way his mind could leap from topic to topic without warning. This time she was immensely grateful for the sudden switch.

The sandy bottom was within reach, allowing her to stand up. Now if only her legs were steadier, Julianna considered, struggling desperately for calm. She glared back at him over her shoulder. "What?"

"If we both end up surrendering at the same time, would it be considered a double defeat? Or a mutual victory?"

Sensing that he was teasing her again, Julianna wasn't about to touch such a dangerous topic.

Instead, she marched away.

Needing to give his aroused body a chance to cool down, Dylan remained behind in the pool.

He floated lazily on his back, watched Julianna stomp out of the water and decided that despite her deceptively slender frame, Julianna Valderian possessed a very lush, aesthetically appealing rear end.

Her clothes were disgustingly dusty. Julianna shook them out, wondering why it was that two highly intelligent individuals such as Dylan and her hadn't thought to rinse them out while bathing. Surely the hot sun would have dried them quickly.

The answer, of course, was all too obvious. They'd both had something else on their minds. Something far more basic and definitely more appealing than laundry.

Feeling his gaze on her, and not wanting to remain naked any longer than necessary, Julianna decided against taking time to wash her dress and thin chemise.

Giving them another swift shake, she told herself that gritty clothing was the proper price to pay for having allowed her uncharacteristically turbulent, distressingly human emotions to rule her always-logical Sarnian head.

She'd just finished pulling the dress over her head and was adjusting the draped folds when she viewed the billowing cloud of dust in the distance.

"Someone's coming!"

"I see them."

If Julianna had been uncomfortable with her state of undress, Dylan displayed no such concern. He waded from the pool, blatantly nude and proudly male.

"Do you think they're bandits?" His casual tone suggested that such an idea brought only curiosity, no fear.

She dragged her reluctantly admiring gaze from his bronze body. "They could be. It is also possible that they are pirates, or assassins, or worse."

Dylan shrugged off her obvious I-told-you-so tone as he proceeded to dress without haste. "We'll handle it."

As irritated as she was by his seemingly indeflatible ego, Julianna liked the way he said *we* and not *I.*

"One of us should have thought to wash these clothes," he muttered, brushing the dust off his trouser legs. He shook out the filthy shirt, frowned, lifted it to his nose, grimaced and tossed it back down to the ground.

"The same thought crossed my mind," Julianna admitted.

"I guess we had other things on our minds." Dylan flashed her one of his quick, sexy grins.

She wasn't even going to attempt to deny it. "Sometimes it's as if you can read my mind."

Still entranced by the sight of his bare chest, and remembering how stimulating those silky black hairs had felt against her bare breasts, Julianna forgot to censor her thoughts.

"I wish it were that easy to read any woman's mind. The truth is, Juls, I can read your eyes."

The very same eyes he was referring to widened in surprise and alarm. "You can?"

"Yep. I'm sure you've been told that they're beautiful hundreds of times."

Actually, she hadn't. Except by her father, of course, but Julianna had always known he found them appealing because they were replicas of her mother's.

When she didn't immediately answer, Dylan took her silence for agreement. "We have a saying on Earth," he said, putting up his hand to shade his eyes as they watched the cloud of swirling red dust draw closer, "about the eyes being the windows to the soul.

"I don't know all that much about souls, but I do know that your eyes give away everything that's going on inside that brilliant, sexy mind of yours."

"That is impossible," Julianna argued. "I have always been exceptional at hiding my thoughts."

"Perhaps with other people—other men—on Sarnia." Dylan glanced over at her. "But not with me."

It was, she admitted reluctantly, the truth. "No. Not with you." Their gazes met and held. Then they smiled.

"I suppose that makes us even," Dylan said.

"How's that?"

"Your eyes give your thoughts away every time. And my body keeps giving mine away every time your luscious lips get within kissing distance. Looks as if we're not going to be able to keep many secrets from one another, Juls."

"I suppose not," she echoed. For some reason, that thought didn't seem nearly as discomfiting as it might have two days ago.

Dylan's smile faded as his gaze moved over her face. "Damn."

"What?"

"I didn't notice under all that dust, but your face is turning as red as this asteroid."

"That would be logical. Since I have spent most of my life beneath the dome of my planet, I have not been exposed to ultraviolet rays for very extended periods of time."

He reached out, ran his fingertip down her cheek. "You're going to be as uncomfortable as hell."

"I'll live."

His smile bloomed anew. "That's the idea." He returned his gaze to the dust cloud. "I've been thinking about what we're going to do next."

"And?"

"And it's obvious that you can't go back to Sarnia."

She looked at him as if he'd just said space was a vacuum.

"Of course I'm going back. It is my home." And she had things to do there. Important things.

"Surely it hasn't slipped that admittedly brilliant mind of yours that you've been banished by the Council of Elders? And that you currently have a death sentence hanging over your lovely blond head?"

Julianna was momentarily distracted by Dylan's assertion that he thought her lovely. He'd told her so in both words and deeds before. But what she found amazing was that she was actually beginning to believe it.

"Sarnians prize honesty," she reminded him. "If I can only return and be heard, my countrymen will be grateful to me for telling them the truth about our planet's origins."

"I wouldn't be so sure of that," Dylan said. He was prepared to argue further when the group who was creating the cloud of red dust crested the dune.

The men were stocky, strong armed and strong limbed, reminding Dylan of Paleolithic Earth humans with their sloping foreheads and overly hairy bodies.

"They are Bardouins," Julianna breathed.

"Is that good? Or bad?"

"Better than I'd feared. As a rule, the nomadic tribes on 229 only fight among themselves."

"So they can be dangerous?"

"Under some circumstances, they can be deadly. Nomadic tribes are the only ones who dare leave the towns and cities and brave the harsh elements. And although they serve a valuable function as traders on the more inhospitable outposts, such as this asteroid, many xenoanthropologists consider them at the bottom of the animal ladder."

"Even below terrans?"

"Yes." She glanced over at Dylan and realized he was teasing her again. "Although one of my professors at the Science Institute once put forth a theory that the nomads could possibly be the missing link between lower-form animals and terrans."

The smile in her eyes told him she was teasing him back, something she wouldn't, couldn't, have done two days ago. They were, Dylan thought with satisfaction, making progress.

"You're always so good for the ego, Juls," he muttered, his own smile softening his words. The nomads had come to a stop about a hundred yards away and had begun to talk among themselves. "I suppose I'd better go talk with them." He put his hand on her arm. "Wait here."

"Of course."

"Of course?" Dylan lifted a brow. "Julianna Valderian suddenly turning acquiescent?" He shot a quick glance upward. "The sky must be falling."

Understanding the humor in his accusation, Julianna was not offended. "Nomads are known to possess very alphalike thought processes. They would never accept a mere woman addressing them."

Although he'd never considered himself a chauvinist, Dylan had, unfortunately, earned Charity's short-lived ire by arguing against her decision to quit her job as a deputy prosecutor in the L.A. district attorney's office to join the Venice, California, police department.

At the time he'd insisted, truthfully, that his grounds had been understandable brotherly concern about his baby sister putting her life on the line every time she donned her blue uniform of authority. Never had he believed her incapable of doing the required police work as well as any of her male counterparts.

"Gloria Steinem would probably not be thrilled to discover that male chauvinism remains alive and well in the twenty-second century," he said now.

As an ardent campaigner for female rights on Sarnia, Julianna recognized the name immediately. The terran feminist had been prominently mentioned in several of the forbidden papers that had gotten her into this mess.

Despite his sometimes frustrating male cockiness, Julianna had to admit that Dylan had proven remarkably egalitarian during their time together.

"Unfortunately, that is true," she agreed, thinking how ironic it was that Sarnians, who'd always considered themselves the most intelligent beings in the galaxy, shared their misguided beliefs of male dominance with those very same individuals they considered the least intelligent.

"And that being the case, these nomads would not respect—or, more importantly, fear—any male who permitted his woman to speak in mixed company," she explained.

His woman. The surge of possessiveness her words instilled was definitely not a familiar emotion. Neither was it all that unappealing, Dylan decided.

He took a deep breath to clear his mind. "Wish me luck."

He wanted to touch a hand to her cheek to reassure her, but mindful of her sunburn, and her statement about male and female roles among the nomads, Dylan resisted. One thing he definitely couldn't afford was to appear weak.

"Good luck, Dylan," she responded, once again taking his words literally.

Julianna watched Dylan approach the group on a slow, easy, nonthreatening, but highly confident stride. He was, she thought on a burst of pride, remarkable. How many men could have handled all the unexpected and dangerous problems Dylan had been forced to deal with since his arrival on Sarnia?

Only one other that she knew of. Starbuck. No wonder they'd become friends, Julianna mused. Dylan and her brother were a great deal alike. Oh, Dylan was far more outgoing and his humor was definitely distracting, but the two men were both rugged, freethinking, heroic individuals. And she cared deeply for them both. In Dylan's case, she considered, probably too much.

All of the women were on foot. A few of the males rode on animals resembling a genetic cross between armored dinosaurs and camels, others were on horses. One, obviously the leader, sat astride a gleaming black stallion that could have held its own at any Arabian horse show back on Earth.

Although they may have resembled early Earth man, Dylan noted that their clothing was worlds different from the rough animal skins worn by his Paleolithic and Neanderthal ancestors. Both the men and women were clad in vivid, flowing garments created of a gauzy, silklike material.

"Good afternoon," he greeted the leader, who was dressed in royal purple and gold. He approached, his hands open and outstretched, revealing that he carried no weapon. The phaser was tucked away in the waistband of his pants, nestled reassuringly against his spine.

Rather than greet him in return, the man hit him with a barrage of questions.

Grateful for the universal translator, Dylan answered, saying that, yes, he was a terran, and, yes, he had been the pilot of the vehicle the nomads had found on their trek across the blazing red desert.

His words created a stir among the mounted men. They talked among themselves for a long, nerve-racking time, their voices too low for Dylan to hear.

Finally, the leader turned back to Dylan, telling him what he definitely hadn't wanted to hear. Word of his and Julianna's escape was already common knowledge throughout the galaxy. The Ruling Council of Elders had offered a generous reward for the pair's return.

He considered assuring them that they had the wrong people, that he and Julianna were merely two innocent space travelers who'd been blown off course during a meteor shower.

But he'd seen the men studying her with great interest during their lengthy conversation and knew that her silvery gown—worn only by the ruling classes on Sarnia—had given her away.

He was trying to decide exactly what to do next when the man's next words practically blew Dylan away. Although the translator couldn't quite keep up with the rapid-fire guttural words, the gist of the leader's remarks seemed to be that they, too, had known the power and the fury of the Sarnian Ruling Council and considered the Elders their blood enemies.

That being the case, the leader of the Bardouin tribe explained, his words accompanied by a vigorous nodding of both male and female heads, they would do everything they could to help Julianna and Dylan escape the death sentence that had been put on their heads.

Julianna watched, her heart in her throat, as Dylan continued to carry on the lengthy conversation with the nomads. Finally, just when she didn't think she could stand the suspense a moment longer, he turned on his heel and headed back toward her, the nomads following behind him.

"What's happening?" she asked when he got within hearing distance.

"I'm not absolutely sure," he said. "But I think we've been invited to dinner."

9

THEY SPENT THE NIGHT at the oasis, invited to sleep in the spacious tent of the leader, his three wives and twelve children. Although the nomad's loud snoring kept him awake most of the night, Dylan was grateful for the company.

Because although he'd promised himself that he wasn't going to make love to Julianna until she asked him to—she wouldn't really have to beg, he'd decided magnanimously—he wasn't certain he could have spent the long night alone in such proximity to her without breaking his vow.

Though the desert night had been cold, morning dawned hot and dry. The sun was barely above the rosy red horizon, yet Dylan guessed that the temperature was already high in the nineties.

It would climb a great deal higher before the day was over. Fortunately, his new friends had assured him that the settlement he was seeking was not that faraway.

"I don't feel at all like myself," Julianna complained, tugging upward on the low, off-the-shoulder neckline of her short gold dress.

Dylan was tying the saddlebags on the horse he'd been given last night after imbibing a prodigious amount of a lethal, alcoholic beverage called Enos Ale with the male nomads.

"My enemy's enemy is my friend," the leader had declared boisterously, giving Dylan a huge bear hug. Then, drawing cheers from his followers, he had bestowed the dappled gray gelding, along with various provisions, upon Dylan with a grand, sweeping gesture.

Ignoring the hangover that had little demons blasting away with laser pistols inside his head, Dylan glanced over at her.

"I think you look great. In fact, all you'd need is a sword and you'd look as if you were ready to go out and slay dragons."

Last night, over an unrecognizable dinner that had tasted a lot like roasted venison and had definitely been superior to the freeze-dried meals on the *Mutiny,* it had been decided that Julianna's gown was a dead giveaway. Fortunately, since the nomads did a brisk business as traders, they had an appropriate costume in stock.

Of course there had been no question of Julianna resisting the masquerade. She was, after all, Dylan had reminded her, sotto voce, as the youngest of the leader's three wives obediently rose and invited Julianna to accompany her to the tent to find an appropriate dress, a mere female.

So her lovely Sarnian gown, which her parents had bought her upon her graduation with honors from the Science Institute had been taken away and burned, leaving her with no choice but to accept the proffered garment.

Which was why she was starting out her day dressed in something Julianna considered more appropriate for one of the voluptuous green prostitutes from the planet Cyprian.

Frowning, she tugged at the hem of the skirt, which ended high on her thigh. In addition to its brevity, she feared the sun would render the woven gold material nearly invisible. Her new sandals were gold, as well, with gilt lacings crisscrossing her bare legs.

"I've never worn anything like this in my life."

Her clothing had always been determined by her family's position in the highly stratified society. White or silver, with the occasional gray or black for formal occasions. The necklines had been properly demure, the flowing sleeves reaching to her wrists. And her legs had always, without exception, been discreetly covered.

"You look terrific," Dylan repeated, thinking the metallic gold cloth reminded him of the molten heat of Julianna's passion. "Except for your face. It's still awfully red."

One of the wives had given her a lotion to spread on her inflamed skin, but it still felt uncomfortably dry.

"Why, thank you for the lovely compliment," she muttered.

"You want compliments?" he asked obligingly.

"Never mind," she said quickly. She'd already discovered, to her dismay, how quickly his smooth, admiring words could undermine her self-control. "I still don't understand why you don't have to change."

"Because I'm already wearing terran clothes," he explained patiently yet again.

Although last night he'd been drunker than a Maine lumberman at spring thaw, he had managed to remember to rinse the captain's black shirt and pants out in the oasis before retiring. And while the cool desert night air had kept the garments from drying completely, he knew that today's blazing sun would soon finish the job.

"And since everyone's looking for a terran man and a Sarnian woman, the idea is for us to pass as a terran couple, remember?"

As she tugged at the neckline for the umpteenth time that morning, Julianna refused to acknowledge that his point was valid.

There was one more thing they had to do before they could leave. But suspecting how Julianna would react, Dylan had waited until the last minute.

When he'd secured the saddlebags, Dylan knew he'd run out of time. He couldn't stall any longer.

"We're almost ready to go."

She could hear the *but* in his voice. "Why do I think I'm not going to like this?"

"Probably because you're not. I'm afraid there's one more thing you have to wear."

She stared at the all-too-familiar piece of hammered gold he was holding out toward her. "I categorically refuse to wear a marriage collar."

"Most females in the galaxy wear marriage collars," Dylan reminded her calmly. "Including Sarnians."

She tossed her head, causing a cloud of pale blond hair to settle over her bare shoulder. That was another thing that was disturbing her: Dylan had not permitted her to put it into its tidy Sarnian braid this morning. Julianna hadn't worn her hair loose since childhood. It felt hot and heavy. Also far too free and vaguely wanton.

"Not this Sarnian female."

"Ah, but that's exactly the point," Dylan reminded her. Frustration was making his hangover worse. His head was pounding, and he felt as if an entire herd of the nomads' ugly dromedarylike beasts had paraded through his mouth during the night. "You're no longer a Sarnian, Juls. You're my terran wife. Remember?"

Wife. There had been a time when another man had wanted her for his wife.

Zoltar Flavius, ambassador to Galactia and a man twice her age, had asked her father for her hand in marriage.

At the coaxing of his terran wife, Xanthus Valderian had agreed to permit Julianna to select her own bond-mate. Which had proven a disastrous political mistake when she refused to even consider a marriage contract with the powerful, wealthy ambassador, who, like Xanthus himself, was descended from the Ancient Ones.

Unfortunately, news of her refusal had spread throughout Sarnia, as well as the rest of the galaxy. Since women were not empowered to choose their own destiny, such freedom was considered abhorrent by old-line conservatives at the same time it was found vastly encouraging by proponents of female rights. Women such as herself.

What she hadn't foreseen was that her freedom of choice would prove Zoltar Flavius's public humiliation. A powerful man with a temper that was decidedly un-Sarnian, he'd effectively gotten Xanthus Valderian removed from the governing body of city states. Julianna had always suspected that her father's forced retirement had been the cause of his fatal heart attack during the past solar year.

Once he'd finished with her father, Zoltar had directed his fury toward his intended bride. But before he could succeed in getting her fired from the institute, on the way back to Galactia his space pod had been hit by a meteor shower, effectively putting an end to both the ambassador's life and his revenge.

Not that she'd escaped entirely unscathed, Julianna considered now. Because she'd always suspected that the spy in her laboratory, the very same assistant who had turned her in to the Ruling Council, had been placed there by Zoltar.

"I have no intention of ever becoming any man's wife," Julianna said now. Marriage made a woman subservient to her male master. Something she'd always vowed never to be.

Dylan swore. He'd never met a more stubborn female. Except, perhaps his sister. Julianna could definitely give Charity a run for her money.

"This isn't a proposal, Juls," he said between gritted teeth. "It's merely a way to try to keep that head on those lovely bare shoulders."

He had a point, she admitted reluctantly. But how could she explain her innate distaste for that hated collar? It represented everything she had spent years quietly and persistently rebelling against.

"We have a custom on Earth," he said, his tone softening. "Perhaps you have read of it. When a man and woman exchange marriage vows, they also exchange rings as a sign of their vow of commitment to one another."

"I know the custom," she murmured. "My parents exchanged such wedding bands." Against logic, her mother still wore hers on the fourth finger of her left hand, claiming that it continued to make her feel close to her late husband.

"But my father wore a ring, as well," she pointed out. And had received a great deal of criticism from his male peers for doing so, too, she remembered. "So their exchange was equal."

For the sake of argument, Julianna conveniently overlooked the fact that her mother had also donned a jeweled gold collar, as custom required.

"Men do not wear marriage collars. Which makes the collar nothing more than a disgusting symbol of slavery."

"Point taken." Dylan's expression was as frustrated as she'd ever seen it. "And believe me, Julianna, I'd never ask you to do anything you honestly couldn't do.

"But this is important. And so long as you and I both know that it's only make-believe, that I'd never consider you, or any other woman to be chattel, how could it hurt to put the damn thing on?"

"I insist on keeping the key." If she did agree to go along with his plan, she refused to hand him total control.

"Fine. Actually, I was intending to give it to you."

His calm, obviously truthful statement took a bit of the mutinous wind out of Julianna's sails. "All right," she said on a frustrated breath of air. "But don't get any ideas."

She was, Dylan decided, as prickly as one of the cacti he'd seen during a visit to the desert section of the

Smithsonian botanical gardens in Washington, D.C. But at least she'd given in.

"I wouldn't think of it," he said agreeably.

She closed her eyes as she felt the metal close around her neck, flinching when she heard the fatal click of the lock.

"All done. That wasn't so bad, was it?"

When she refused to answer, Dylan took her hand, which was clenched into a fist at her side, uncurled her fingers and pressed the brass key into her palm.

Beneath the gold dress, she was wearing an uncomfortable garment that cupped her breasts, elevating them and thrusting them together in way she found embarrassingly scandalous. Wanting to keep the all-important key safe, she quickly stuck it in her cleavage.

As he watched the shiny brass key disappear between the soft ivory globes of her breasts, Dylan knew that Julianna was not a woman to flaunt her sensuality. That being the case, he also realized that her action was unconsciously seductive. But that knowledge didn't stop the urgent heat from rushing into his groin. "Now that we've got that little matter settled, we'd better get this show on the road. Before the sun gets any higher."

As Dylan marched back to the horse with long, strangely brusque strides, Julianna wondered what had happened to change his mood so suddenly. He'd gotten what he wanted. So why was he suddenly behaving as unsociable as a Janurian pit viper?

Deciding that she'd never completely understand the enigma that was the terran male mind, Julianna dragged her hand frustratedly through her loosened hair and followed him.

Distances, Dylan discovered, were obviously relative on 229. Although the nomad chief had assured him that the settlement was near, it proved to be almost another long day's journey.

Fortunately, today they were able to ride rather than walk. After they'd gotten beyond sight of the nomad's camp, he'd lifted Julianna astride the gelding and set her down in front of him. And although he supposed that riding was a lot better than trekking across the miles of hot red sand on foot, the feel of Julianna's round little rear pressing intimately against his groin did nothing to soothe either Dylan's body or his mind.

They stopped for a brief lunch of meat and cheeses, drinking from the saddlebags filled with water. Fortunately, the herbal sunscreen lotion the nomads had given them seemed to be working, keeping Julianna's exposed skin from burning any more.

At the outskirts of the ragtag batch of red stone buildings, Dylan pulled the reins to bring the horse to a halt. "You'd better get down," he said.

She understood that they would call less attention to themselves if she walked beside him into town, like a proper wife. Even knowing that, she was reluctant to get down from the horse. Because although she'd die before admitting it, Julianna had quite enjoyed the feel of his hard male body pressed so intimately against her during the long, dusty ride.

"Now that we've reached civilization, what do you suggest we do next?"

"Figure out a way to get our hands on some diamaziman crystals so we can get the hell of this place and get to Earth."

The carbon-based stone whose atoms had been crystallized into a solid cubic pattern had long been utilized on Sarnia to beam down visitors who did not possess the ability of astro-projection.

"We?"

"We. As in you and I."

"I understand the word," she said with that coolness that she'd tried to make him believe was second nature. "But I cannot go to Earth. I told you," she insisted, "I must return to Sarnia. It's important that people know the truth."

Her mission would, Julianna thought with a complete lack of Sarnian modesty, change the life of every woman on her planet.

Dylan had absolutely no intention of allowing Julianna to risk her life. But knowing exactly how stubborn she could be, he decided to put off the argument as long as possible.

"How about a compromise?"

"What kind of compromise?" It had not escaped her notice that such bargains, which initially sounded quite equable, invariably ended up favoring him.

"Why don't we discuss this after we get the crystals?" he suggested.

"It won't be easy," she reported as they made their way down the red dirt street that was the main thoroughfare of the outpost settlement.

It was obvious that the town had not been planned by committee. The various rough-hewn buildings, some quite decrepit, had been erected in a haphazard fashion, displaying no continuity of design or interest in aesthetics.

"Diamaziman is valuable. I doubt that there are any on this asteroid. And the nearest planet the crystal is mined is Uriah."

"So that's where we'll go." The street was deserted. Obviously the residents were smart enough to stay indoors during the hot afternoon hours.

"How do you suggest doing that? When we possess no craft and neither one of us possesses Starbuck's astro-projection capabilities?"

"We'll figure out something."

He reined in the gelding in front of a building whose red rock facade boasted not a single window. Interestingly, entrance to the building was through a pair of swinging doors.

"Is this place what I think it is?"

She read the sign above the door. "It is a tavern." Her tone held her opinion of such an unsavory establishment.

"Terrific." Dylan dismounted and tied the reins to what resembled a hitching post in all those John Wayne Westerns he enjoyed on the late, late shows.

She caught his sleeve as he turned toward the door. "You're not going in there?"

"That's the plan."

"But why?"

"In the first place, it's the best place in town to pick up local gossip. We can probably find out the latest info on our escapee status.

"And in the second place, I need a drink."

"I would have thought you'd imbibed enough alcohol last night."

In the sake of peace, he ignored her censorious tone. "Haven't you ever heard of the hair of the dog?"

"No."

"I'll explain it later," Dylan promised. "Over a tall icy mug of Enos Ale. Let's go."

"Surely you don't expect me to go in there?"

"I sure as hell don't intend to leave you out here alone," Dylan answered. "So, yeah, I guess the only thing for you to do is come with me."

She dug in her heels, both physically and figuratively. "I've never been a tavern."

"Then this will be another in a long line of recent first-time experiences."

How could she make him understand? "Properly brought up Sarnian women do not frequent taverns."

"You're not a Sarnian, damn it," he reminded her. "You're a terran. And you're my wife." He glanced toward a trio of men walking down the dusty street toward the tavern. "And properly brought up terran wives do not argue with their husbands in public."

His hand cupped her elbow, he leaned down so their faces were close together. "It's important that we pull off this charade, Juls. You could even call it a life-or-death performance. So, are you coming with me quietly, or do I have to put on the chain and drag you in there?"

One of the most humiliating things about the marriage collar was the single loop that allowed a chain to be attached. Men who loved and respected their wives—honorable, loving men such as her father—

would never think of resorting to such degrading behavior.

"You wouldn't!"

Her eyes blazed as gold as her metallic dress and her lips were trembling in obvious outrage. The rest of Julianna was trembling as well. She was furious at his threat and making absolutely no attempt to hide it.

"Try me."

She stared up at him incredulously. "This is another one of your terran jokes, isn't it? You're teasing me again. Despite our short time together, I know you, Dylan Prescott. You'd never put me on a chain."

Dylan merely shrugged. Of course he wouldn't. But he was afraid that if he allowed Julianna to walk all over him, she might get too cocky and end up putting them in even worse danger.

"If I were you, I wouldn't put it to a test."

Her eyes narrowed. She refused to believe he was serious.

"Are you coming?" he asked into the thick silence swirling around them. "Or are you going to force me to drag you in there like a disobedient German shepherd puppy?"

Reluctantly Julianna made her choice. "All right. But I am only going under protest." And then she brushed past him with a remarkably haughty attitude for a woman with every policeman, pirate and bounty hunter in the galaxy looking for her.

"Protest noted," Dylan ground out.

The single rectangular room was as dark as the bottom of a coal mine. Dylan stood with Julianna in the entrance, allowing his eyes to adjust to the change in light, realizing that they were the center of attention and unable to do anything about it.

As his pupils gradually dilated, he saw that the bar wasn't all that different from the waterfront bar where Starbuck had created such a ruckus during his misguided attempt to rescue Charity.

The interior walls were the same rough red rock as the exterior of the building. Tables, created from some type of twenty-second century Formica-like material were scattered around the dirt floor. Through the haze of smoke drifting upward, Dylan realized that the clientele was definitely worlds away from the beer and bourbon drinkers at Castle Mountain's The Stewed Clam.

Spotting a table at the back of the room, he led her to it, weaving their way past the interested onlookers. "Don't say a word to anyone. And don't move," he instructed.

Julianna nodded, her attention drawn to a nearby table where a voluptuous green Cyprian prostitute was sitting on a ridge-headed Janurian's lap, doing remarkable things with her pointed tongue in his ear.

Initial distaste was overrun by intellectual curiosity as she realized that never had she seen such a wealth of different species in one place. This tavern was an xenoanthropologist's dream.

Dylan made his way back to the bar, where a reptilian humanoid with scaly skin that kept turning from green to silver and back again took his order. He ordered a flagon of Enos Ale for himself and, pointing at a green bottle, ordered something that resembled white wine for Julianna.

"I forgot to ask you what you wanted," he said when he returned to the table.

Julianna took a tentative sip of the pale gold liquid, finding it crisp and dry on the tongue. "This is quite pleasurable."

"I'm glad you like it." Now that he'd gotten his way, he could afford to be magnanimous. Dylan took a drink of the icy brew that was stronger than the domestic beer he was accustomed to drinking back home.

Feeling the ale go to work on his headache, he leaned back in his chair, his eyes sweeping the room with interest. Every species in the galaxy must be represented, he decided.

For the first time since he'd landed on Sarnia, Dylan allowed himself the luxury of observing his environment with a curious interest that had nothing to do with the deadly situation he'd found himself in.

Starbuck had filled him in on some of the news of the future. Dylan had been encouraged to learn that Earth was still spinning two hundred years later, that its residents hadn't blown it up or polluted it out of existence.

He knew that California had not yet dropped into the sea but a major earthquake was expected anytime. Earth's forests, unfortunately, no longer existed. Although third- and fourth-growth forests had been farmed, eventually the harvesting became too expensive and wood products were replaced by superior amalgams.

When Dylan had heard that unhappy news, he'd decided that was definitely a case where meddling in the future was not only permitted but necessary.

He'd been gratified to discover that a collation of government and private enterprise solved the homeless problem in the twenty-first century. And the United States had had five female presidents. Starbuck had mentioned that Julianna often included this encouraging statistic in her women's rights speeches on Sarnia.

The New York Yankees were still on a losing streak, but Starbuck had assured him that the team had a new owner, so fans were hopeful.

Although Starbuck had told him much about this faraway time and place during their time working together in the lab, Dylan's mind was filled with questions. Now the trick would be in living long enough to learn all the answers.

"This reminds me of the bar scene in *Star Wars*."

"It does, doesn't it?"

He glanced over the rim of his pewter mug at her, curious. "You know about *Star Wars*?"

"The terran film," she replied mildly, observing a pair of eight-armed Arachnidians playing some sort of game with a double deck of cards. "Although the Council of Arts declared the films illogical and banned their distribution on Sarnia more than fifty solar revolutions ago, a hard-core group of fans such as myself remain. So Federation traders smuggle them past customs to supply a very efficient black market."

"Amazing." Dylan shook his head, wondering what other Earth cultures had survived the centuries. He also found it astonishing that Julianna, that upstanding proponent of truth and honesty, would break the law by dealing with black marketeers. No wonder she knew so much about transport pilots.

"I've always found the *Star Wars* trilogy quite entertaining," Julianna said. "Although to be perfectly honest, I much prefer the *Star Trek* series."

As he looked at Julianna across the table, his gaze focused on her hands. Her fingers, curled around the stem of her glass were long and lean and pale. Remembering how they'd felt against his body caused that now-familiar curling of desire deep in his gut.

And as he thought about how much he wanted Julianna, another thought, as outrageous as it was unbidden, leaped into his unruly mind.

What if, instead of returning to Earth, he stayed in this galaxy and this time? He'd always been a reasonably adaptable individual. How hard could it be to learn to eat as the people around him ate, drink as they drank, live as they lived?

Wouldn't it be worth it? So long as he could be with Julianna?

"Too bad there's not a jukebox," he said, glancing around the smoky room.

"A jukebox?"

"A machine that makes music," Dylan explained. "I feel like dancing."

"Dancing?"

For not the first time since meeting her, Dylan decided that Sarnia wasn't exactly a fun planet. No wonder Starbuck had chosen to remain on Earth with Charity.

"It's a little difficult to explain," he said. "A man holds a woman in his arms, and they move in time to the music."

"And this is enjoyable?"

"Extremely. With the right partner." Dylan wondered what she'd say if he told her the kind of dancing he had in mind was a lot closer to foreplay than fox-trot.

Then, as had happened so many times before, their eyes met across the table, their thoughts tangled, and Dylan knew, without a single doubt, that despite her brother's claim that Julianna lacked the gift of extrasensory perception, she was reading his mind.

Her cheeks, still tinted pink by yesterday's sun, blazed an even darker scarlet.

"Juls—"

His attention shifting to her slightly parted lips, Dylan neglected to see the individual approaching until he was standing at their table.

"I haven't seen you here before," the stranger said to Dylan.

The man was dressed in an orange flight suit, allowing Dylan to recognize him as a transport pilot. More pirate than pilot, Dylan decided, taking in the man's eyes, which were as hard as the aggie shooter he'd once used to win a childhood marble tournament.

"That's probably because we haven't been here before," Dylan said easily. "There's not all that much to do on an out-of-the-way hellhole like 229."

"True enough." Without waiting for an invitation, the man pulled out a chair, turned it around and straddled it. "But I wouldn't think boredom would be much of a problem for you." His hard dark gaze moved from Dylan to Julianna. "Not with this female to bed."

His eyes, as they swept over her body, felt like clammy hands. How strange it was that when Dylan looked at her in much the same way, she felt warmth flooding through her veins rather than this uncomfortable chill, Julianna mused.

Dylan felt Julianna's discomfort. Beneath the table, he put a soothing hand on her bare knee. "Something I can do for you?" he asked the pilot.

"You can sell me your woman."

Since he'd already gotten a pretty good idea of how things worked on 229, Dylan was not all that surprised by what, only a few days ago, would have seemed an unbelievable suggestion.

"Sorry." He took another drink of ale. "I doubt you could afford her."

The man threw a gleaming gold coin onto the table. "That should cover the first night." His teeth flashed in a predator's grin, reminding Dylan of a wolf. "After one night with me, she won't need—or want—any other bed partners."

"You sound pretty sure of yourself."

"I'm sure of this."

When the man grabbed his crotch in an obscene gesture, Dylan felt Julianna begin to tremble beside him. Knowing that her reaction was born of fury, not fear, he tightened his fingers warningly on her knee.

"A good woman is hard to find," Dylan pointed out. "Besides, I've put a great deal of time in training the wench properly. One lousy gold coin isn't sufficient repayment for my efforts."

Instead of appearing offended, the man threw back his head and laughed. "You drive a hard bargain, my friend." He tossed a leather bag into the center of the table. "There's a Sarnian Elder's ransom in diamaziman in that bag," he said.

"Stolen diamaziman," Dylan guessed.

The pilot shrugged. "The previous owner died unexpectedly. He had no further use for it."

Dylan had a very good idea how the unfortunate individual died. The diamaziman crystals he and Julianna needed so badly were there, right in front of him. Dylan wondered exactly how to go about getting it.

"It should be more than enough to cover your time and expenses," the pilot said.

He stood up, came around the table and ran a finger along Julianna's neck, above the gold collar. His nails were filthy, she noted with an inner cringe, underneath caked with what appeared to be at least a month's worth of dark red dirt.

"After all," the man continued to bargain, "in the dark, one female is much like another. And you can always buy yourself another wife."

He grinned again. "A younger one, perhaps. With those crystals, you could probably even afford a virgin. Not a terran, perhaps. But Kliranian girls are nearly as succulent. And they enjoy pain." This time his wicked smile made Dylan's flesh crawl.

If this unprincipled savage was any example of a typical terran transport pilot, it was no wonder Julianna had greeted him with such loathing, Dylan decided.

"Your offer is tempting," he said slowly.

"Tempting?" Julianna's voice climbed at least an octave higher than its normal throaty pitch. "Are you actually going to sit there and bargain for me as if I'm no better than—" she tossed her head in the direction of the Cyprian prostitute, who was now straddling the Janurian's thighs in a most provocative manner "—her?"

"That's enough, woman," Dylan snapped, giving Julianna a harsh, warning look.

She ignored him. "It's not nearly enough."

His fingers tightened hard enough to leave bruises on her thigh. "Shut that female mouth or I will shut it for you."

Brushing aside his hand, she stood up, knocking her chair over behind her. "Don't you dare tell me to be quiet!" She now had the attention of everyone in the bar. "And as for you . . ."

She stood in front of the startled transport pilot and began jabbing a finger in his chest. "You have absolutely no right to speak of a woman in such a demeaning fashion."

"Damn it, Juls," Dylan muttered, "let it go."

But Julianna was on a roll. "I've let it go all my life," she spat out. "And look where it's gotten me. I'm tired of keeping quiet while inferior men are given privileges the average female wouldn't dare dream of.

"I'm sick of being a second-class citizen on my own planet. And I'm fed up with males strutting around as if they own the galaxy, simply because they happened to be born with their sex organs on the outside of their bodies, rather than the inside."

She'd managed a direct hit to the pilot's ego with that one. His fingers curled around her wrist. "You want to feel a male organ, bitch?"

Dylan cursed as he watched Julianna being dragged against the pilot's aroused body. Despite his college pugilistic training, he'd always considered himself a lover, not a fighter. Unfortunately, Julianna had given him no choice.

But before he could intercede, Julianna managed to get one arm free. Swinging with all her might, she landed her fist right in the center of the pilot's face. And then, for good measure, she got him again, hard, in the crotch with her knee.

Bellowing like a bull moose calling for his mate, the terran fell to the ground, one hand clutching his injured sex, the other pressed over his nose.

The sight of the pilot rolling over the floor, blood spurting darkly from between his fingers galvanized every male in the bar to action.

The Janurian at the next table dumped the prostitute onto the red dirt floor and left his chair as if ejected from it. Other men followed.

All hell broke loose.

Tables were overturned, glasses spilled as blows were enthusiastically exchanged. It was, Julianna considered, staring at the melee surrounding her, as if grateful for any diversion, the men didn't much care who they hit, so long as they managed to connect with someone.

The entire room was in motion and soon the smoky air was filled with the thudding sound of fists meeting flesh in long punches and short jabs, curses and deep, guttural grunts.

Dylan found himself facedown on the floor, caught up in a tangle of steely arms that were wrapped around him like a python's deadly grip. Something—either a fist or a boot—slammed into his ribs. Pain exploded, his stomach roiled.

When Julianna saw Dylan caught in the grasp of the eight-armed Arachnidian, she grabbed the bottle the Janurian had left behind on the table. She swung it down with all her strength, shattering it over the attacker's head.

A red haze had covered Dylan's eyes. Just when he thought he was going to pass out, he felt the arms loosen. And then, miraculously, he was free.

"If you have imbibed sufficient ale, I would suggest we leave now," Julianna suggested on a cool voice.

"Good idea."

Deciding that a much-needed lecture about holding one's temper in dangerous situations could come later, Dylan pushed himself to his feet. He swayed, grabbed the back of one of the few chairs still standing upright and shook his head to clear the mists shimmering in front of his eyes.

He took her hand, prepared to get the hell out of there when he remembered the diamaziman.

"Don't forget the bag of crystals."

"But that's stealing."

Did she have to argue every little point? Dylan felt himself grinding his teeth again and decided that it would be a miracle if he arrived back on Earth with his molars intact.

"The guy stole the stuff from its original owner in the first place," he reminded her. "This is only poetic justice." It was also their ticket home.

Such reasoning made some semblance of sense, Julianna decided. Snatching up the leather bag, she allowed Dylan to lead her through the teeming mass of male humanity.

Once outside, he pulled her aboard the waiting gelding and together they raced hell-bent for leather down the dusty red street.

10

IT WAS NEARLY DUSK by the time Dylan and Julianna stopped riding. They'd reached another outpost and from what Dylan could tell, they'd managed to leave their pursuers far behind them.

Saying a silent thank-you to the nomad chief for having given him such a fast horse, Dylan reined the gray gelding up in front of what appeared to be yet another tavern.

"Surely you don't need more hair of the dog," Julianna commented with overt disapproval.

"It wouldn't hurt, given the fact that every part of my body is aching from that damn brawl you started," he growled. They were the first words either of them had spoken since escaping the distant town. "But my plan is to ask where we can rent a room for the night. Unless you want to sleep out here in the street."

"We could keep riding," she suggested, glancing nervously back over her shoulder as if expecting to see hoards of armed pirates descending on them at any moment.

"That's not an option." His curt tone said the subject was closed. "Wait here, I'll be right back."

"Don't you want me to come with you?"

"The last time I took you into a bar, you started World War III," he reminded her. "And although I've never considered myself a coward, since there's probably not an inch of flesh on my aching body that isn't turning black-and-blue as we speak, I think I'll leave you out here, where, hopefully, you can't get into too much trouble."

His tone, as well as his words, were highly unflattering. But taking in his swollen jaw, split lip and the unsightly purplish blue shadow beneath his left eye, Julianna decided, for the sake of discretion, not to argue.

"I will be waiting right here when you return," she promised with uncharacteristic meekness.

He muttered something, swung down from the horse and limped toward the door. She noticed, with some interest, that as he entered, he straightened, appearing far more hale and hearty than she suspected him to be at the moment.

A minute turned into two. Then five. Then ten. Julianna was beginning to worry. She was also reconsidering her promise to remain outside. What if Dylan were in trouble? If anything, this scattered grouping of ramshackle buildings appeared even more disreputable than the earlier ones. What if he'd been taken captive? Or worse yet, killed?

She had just about decided to go into the tavern herself, to ensure that Dylan was safe when he came striding out.

The sun was setting on the horizon, creating a fan of gold and crimson light behind her flowing silvery blond hair. Dylan couldn't miss the look of absolute relief on her face.

"Don't tell me that you were worried about me, Juls?"

"Yes." Her eyes met his with not an ounce of guile. "When you didn't immediately return, I become frantic thinking of all the things that might have happened to you in that awful place."

His earlier irritation diminishing somewhat, Dylan reached up and lifted her down from the gelding's high back. "I think I kind of like the idea of you worrying about me."

His fingers were wrapped around her waist. Her hands were on his shoulders. Their thighs were touching, their lips close.

"I got us a room." He brushed an errant strand of blond hair from her cheek. "With a tub."

She smiled and leaned even closer. "A tub?"

Realizing that Julianna was accustomed to the type of sonic shower that was in the lavatory facilities on the *Mutiny,* Dylan said, "To bathe in. Like the oasis."

"That sounds wonderful. I am surprised that there would be any water to spare," she said.

"That was my first thought. But the tavern's built atop a thermal spring," Dylan explained. "The bartender told me he'd drilled a well last month."

"Our timing is fortunate."

"For once," Dylan agreed. "Oh, and there's a bed." He waited for another argument about which one of them would sleep on the floor.

Her back still aching slightly from sleeping on the ground last night, Julianna merely said, "A bed sounds sublime."

Her smile created a renewed flow of heat that nearly had Dylan forgetting his promise to make her beg.

"Then let's go." He released her so fast she nearly stumbled, then turned to retrieve the saddlebags.

"Go where?"

"The guy who owns the bar turned out to be the town's only innkeeper," he informed her. "The rooms are above the tavern. He admits the place isn't fancy, but promised hot water and clean sheets.

"He also promised to take care of the horse in his stable. Oh, and if anyone comes looking for us, he's agreed not to have seen any newcomers for days."

"That's very kind of him," Julianna said.

"I wouldn't exactly go handing the guy the Mother Theresa of the month award," Dylan said dryly. "It's costing us some of the crystals."

Once again, as he'd negotiated with the terran bartender, Dylan had been forced to consider exactly how greedy human beings had become, at least on this galaxy. Never having been all that interested in money himself—except, of course, he allowed, when he was struggling to garner funds for his quantum jump time travel theory—he could only hope such avarice wasn't a universal trend in the twenty-second century.

"They weren't really ours in the first place," she said with a shrug. "Surely you have sufficient left for our purposes."

"Of course. Along with enough to serve as a stake in the monthly big-stakes poker game."

"Poker game?"

"Well, it's not exactly poker," Dylan said. "But according to the bartender, it's close enough to five-card draw that I figure I can do okay."

He was headed toward a set of stairs on the side of the tavern, Julianna close on his heels. "Are you saying that you're actually intending to enter into some game of chance? With our crystals?"

"That's precisely what I'm saying."

"But why?"

"Because we need a way off this asteroid," he reminded her.

"That's what the crystals are for."

"They aren't any good without an accelerator and a computer," Dylan reminded her.

"That is regrettably true. But I still do not understand how you intend to solve that problem by risking our diamaziman crystals."

"Juls." Dylan stopped at the landing at the top of the stairs and turned toward her. "Can we please argue about this later? I'm really not up to a long, drawn-out explanation."

Especially when he didn't have a plan. But something had been teasing at his mind since they'd ridden into town, and as his Grandmother Prescott was always saying, nothing ventured, nothing gained.

"You can be a very frustrating man sometimes, Dylan Prescott," Julianna complained.

"And you can be a very annoying woman, Julianna Valderian." He bent his head and brushed his lips in a friendly fashion against hers. "But I promise not to hold that against you."

The room was as rustic as promised. The floor was red stone, as were the interior walls. The furniture consisted of only a bed, a sagging overstuffed chair that reminded him vaguely of the one his grandfather had spent so many happy evening hours in, and a row of open metal shelves in lieu of a closet.

Through the open doorway, he could see into the adjoining bathroom. Throwing the saddlebags onto the floor beside the bed, he went into the bathroom and turned the taps. As he watched the steam rise from the running water, Dylan decided it was the most beautiful sight—other than Julianna nude—that he'd ever seen.

"Ladies first," he offered even as he yearned to lower his sore body into the hot steamy water.

"You are the one who was forced to fight," Julianna insisted. "A hot bath should be beneficial to your injuries." With a forwardness that she never would have considered three days ago, she began loosening the laces on his black shirt. "Let me help you out of these clothes."

"I think that's supposed to be my line," Dylan drawled as she peeled the material back.

"Oh! You look horrible," she gasped, taking in the sight of the harsh purple bruises spread across his bare chest.

"You know, Juls, there are times when you're awfully tough on a guy's ego."

She lifted her eyes from his battered chest, met his amused eyes that then flared with desire, and acknowledged—to herself—that she *would* be willing to beg. If that's what it took.

But when those burning blue eyes drifted to her lips, Julianna decided that she wouldn't have to.

"I can't believe your ego is in danger of being wounded. Surely a man of your intelligence knows that his body is a magnificent specimen of terran male," she said, treating him to a slow, seductive appraisal.

"Magnificent?"

She nodded. "Absolutely. It was the bruises that I find distasteful." She also felt horribly guilty. She ran her fingertips lightly over his battered rib cage.

Dylan drew in a sharp breath.

Her hands flew off his flesh as if burned. "I'm sorry. Did that hurt?"

"Not in the way you think." He trailed the back of his hand down her cheek. "There is nothing in all the worlds," he murmured, watching the soft blush bloom, "as beautiful as a woman's physical response to her own sensuality." The rosy hue spread from her cheeks to her breasts displayed so provocatively by the clinging minidress. "We have a custom in my world."

Desire had made her lips go as dry as the crimson desert sand outside this steamy, intimate room. "I know," she managed on a husky voice that was little more than a whisper, thinking he was talking about sex again.

Dylan knew what she wanted. But, wanting her first time to be special, he also knew he could wait.

"When someone is injured, a kiss, from the right person, is believed to ease the pain."

Such a belief was surely nothing more than superstition. But as she obliged him by pressing her lips lightly against one of the more virulent bruises, Julianna decided that it was a very nice superstition.

"Like this?"

Dylan leaned his head back and closed his eyes as her mouth left a burning brand against his skin. "Exactly."

She pushed the shirt off his shoulders. "Poor Dylan," she murmured silkily, going up on her toes to kiss a blue mark on his shoulder, "you have a great many injuries." Her tongue cut a wet swath through his chest hair. "It may take all night to tend to them."

He grabbed hold of her hair, gathering it into his fists. "With any luck," he agreed roughly.

She tilted her head back and gave him a slow, secret smile. "Perhaps," she suggested, looking up at him with that unique combination of innocence and blatant sensuality that Dylan had never witnessed in any other woman, "we should take off the rest of your clothes, as well. To check for injuries."

He was being expertly seduced. That, by itself, would have been eminently enjoyable. What made the entire scenario so extraordinary was that the woman doing the seducing was his supposedly logical, cool Julianna.

"Sweetheart," he said, "I thought you'd never ask." He caught her hand as it went to his waist. "On one condition."

Her fingers paused on the fastener of the trousers. "What condition is that?"

"I get to undress you."

She laughed at that, a soft, silvery sound that reminded him of the wind chimes Charity had hung outside her kitchen window back home. "Dispensing with one's clothing is only logical before bathing."

"Let's hear it for logic." Dylan slipped the gilt material off her shoulders. It clung for a brief, tantalizing moment to the curve of her breasts, before slipping the rest of the way to the floor, where it lay in a shimmering gold pool beside his black shirt.

Beneath the dress, she was wearing a matching gold teddy that looked as though it had come from the *Victoria's Secrets* catalogue. Dylan decided it was nice to know that even in the twenty-second century, women—and, conversely, men—were still enamored with sexy lingerie.

"Wonder Woman, eat your heart out," he murmured.

Julianna did not understand his words, but Dylan's meaning was crystallite clear. She stood there, clad solely in the clinging gold undergarment and gilt lace-up sandals, feeling inordinately proud, for the first time in her life, to be totally female.

Without a word, she pulled his trousers down, stopped momentarily by his boots. Kneeling, she tugged off each dusty ebony boot, removed the black pants, one leg at a time, then stood again, her hands on his shoulders, her eyes looking directly into his, filled with invitation.

Dylan did not disappoint. "My turn."

She'd expected him to push the straps of her unfamiliar undergarment off her shoulders, in the same way he had her dress. But yet again, he proved to be a man of surprises. He wet his finger with his tongue and traced a tantalizing line along the voluptuous curve of her breast.

As her nipples pebbled tightly beneath the gold silk, Julianna was surprised that steam wasn't rising from her heated flesh, as well as the tub.

His palms cupped her slender waist, his fingers spanning it effortlessly. She knew he could feel her excited trembling as those wonderful hands moved lower, cupping the rounded curves of her bottom.

Bracing his legs, he bent his head and slanted his mouth over hers. "I can't wait any longer, Juls. I want to make love to you."

Heat uncoiled, penetrated, surrounded her. "Although I know it's wrong, perhaps even wicked, to feel this way," Julianna said on a rippling little sigh, "I want that too."

Her admission felt like a soft summer breeze against his lips. "It isn't wrong. And it certainly isn't wicked," he said, punctuating each word with soft, tender kisses. On the contrary, nothing had ever felt so right in his life.

She was so soft. So sweet. So vulnerable, he reminded himself, despite her amazingly innate sensuality. With unerring accuracy, her fingers stroked a circle around the hard nipple hidden in his black chest hair.

"I'm trying to take things slowly, love," he said on a gritty voice. "But if you keep touching me like that, I can't guarantee that this will last as long as it should. The first time."

"You don't need to go slowly on my account, Dylan," she breathed, tilting her head back, giving his roving lips access to her throat.

She was filled with a potent desire she could not intellectualize away. She was burning from the inside out; Julianna feared that if she didn't soon learn the erotic secrets this man could teach her, she would explode in a fireball of spontaneous combustion.

"Anticipation is half the fun," Dylan managed on a low, rough tone, trying to keep his mind on what he was saying at the same time his body was becoming more and more distracted by her unconscious circular pelvic movement against him.

His hand moved between them, over her rib cage, across her stomach, then lower, still. When he pressed his palm against her, a low moan slipped from between her parted lips.

He undid the tiny snaps at the narrow scrap of gilt silk between her thighs, and discovering the moistness it covered, he parted the sensitive pink flesh, eased his fingers into her, at the same time his tongue embraced the dark cavern of her mouth.

"You're so tight. And warm. And wet."

"I'm sorry, I can't seem to help that," she apologized on a half whisper, half moan.

"Don't ever apologize for wanting me. You're wonderful, Julianna. Just the way you are."

His deep, lusty kiss, and his intimate touch sent a shudder of excitement coursing through her. "Oh, please."

Forgetting his wounds, she clung to him, her unadorned fingernails digging deeply into the warm flesh of his shoulders. She knew she was begging, heard her own voice sound remarkably like a whimper, but didn't care.

"I want . . . I need . . ." For all her knowledge of foreign languages, Julianna knew no words for such rising, desperate feelings.

"I know." As his fingers, probing deeper inside her warm body, encountered resistance, Dylan retreated.

"I need you, too, sweetheart. But our water's getting cold."

Remarkably, she'd forgotten. "I was going to soothe your wounds."

Dylan was far from soothed. "Later," he suggested. With an effort, he reminded himself that he wanted a great deal more from Julianna than a quick roll in the hay. Or, in this case, the bath.

With a series of quick movements, he stripped the silken garment from her. The brass key, which she'd hidden between her breasts this morning, fell to the floor. When Dylan would have bent to pick it up, Julianna stopped him by grabbing his upper arms.

"No," she surprised him by saying. "I want to leave it on." What she couldn't explain, since she didn't even entirely understand it herself, was that on some distant level the gold collar represented her commitment to this one man. For the first time since her father's death, Julianna could finally understand her mother's unwillingness to part with her wedding band.

He knelt to unlace her sandals, then finally kicked off his own too-snug briefs.

Finally entirely undressed, they stood there, inches apart, and found each other wonderful.

And then she felt herself lowered into the tub. Despite his remark to the contrary, the water was far from chilled. "I thought we'd agreed that you would bathe first."

"Actually, I thought I'd join you," Dylan said, with that slow, wicked smile that had her forgetting all the reasons why a future with this man would be absolutely impossible. "To save water."

She nodded. "I am always amazed at how logical the terran mind can be."

"We have our moments." He climbed into the tub, sitting at the opposite end, his feet braced on either side of her hips. "Now," he said, handing her the white bar that smelled remarkably like the soap he was accustomed to using back home, "go ahead and soothe away."

For the next twenty minutes, they took turns driving each other mad. Dylan had to grit his teeth when her slick, soapy palms massaged the inside of his thighs; Julianna thought for sure she'd sink beneath the water and drown when he spread the fragrant white lather over both her breasts, then blew the lather off her nipples with a breath as hot and disturbing as a desert sirocco.

Finally, despite the rising heat of their desire, the bath began to cool. Scooping her into his arms, Dylan lifted her from the velvet cling of water, and, utilizing the last vestiges of his self-control, forced himself to rub them both dry before taking her hand and walking with her to the bed.

"Do you know how long I've been waiting for this moment?" he asked her.

"Three long days?" Dylan would have had to have been deaf not to hear the faint note of self-censure in her tone.

"No." Understanding how difficult it must be for Julianna to behave in such a rash fashion, he brushed his thumb across her suddenly down-turned lips and sought to reassure her. "I've been waiting for this all my life. And two hundred additional years I didn't even know existed, until I landed on your doorstep."

She remembered the old-fashioned bound books her mother had stashed away, romantic terran novels Julianna had always pretended to find silly and illogical, even while she read them late at night, in secret, beneath the covers in the yellow glow of a small laser penlight.

In most of those stories, she recalled, women longed to hear words of encouragement at times like this. They needed to know that they were unique. Special.

And now, as his warm gaze and flattering words sought to reassure, Julianna suspected that Dylan was merely behaving in the gentlemanly manner prescribed by his culture.

She reached up and combed her fingers through his still wet hair. "You don't have to say the words," she murmured. "I don't need them."

"Perhaps not." In turn, he touched his hand to her hair, which streamed wetly over her bare shoulders. "But I need to say them."

Dylan's touch was like a feathery brand, leaving sparks of flame down her neck, along the gold rim of the marriage collar and then over her shoulders. He brushed his lips lightly, reassuringly over hers, then lowered them to her breasts, licking and sucking and biting, until her legs had turned to water and she had to cling to him to keep from sinking to the floor.

The next thing she knew, she was in his arms, lying on her back on the mattress, while he stroked and plundered, pleasured and gave. With hands and lips and words, he peeled away layer after layer of her lingering reserve until she was all raw, quivering emotion.

"Please," she said again, her voice shimmering with a dizzying mixture of pleasure and pain, "I want to know how to please you."

"You please me." His dark head was burrowed between her breasts, his knee nestled snugly between her thighs, his fingers stroking the soft pink petals that guarded her feminine secrets.

Loath to leave his seductive touch, Julianna nevertheless pulled away and went up on her knees beside him. "But I want to know everything," she insisted. "I want to know how to make you burn, the way you do me. If fate decrees that this be the only time we make love, I want to remember this night for all eternity."

Her words set off warning alarms inside his head. "It's not going to be the only time."

"You don't know that," she argued softly.

Dylan's square jaw jutted forward. "Yes, I do." But, unable to resist the appeal in her remarkable golden eyes, he took her slender hand and placed it against his chest. "You will. Lesson number one."

Outside the room, the moon rose high in the midnight dark sky, its cool light slipping past the cracks in the window shutters, bathing the lovers in a soft, silvery light.

Inside the room, Julianna learned all Dylan's secrets, as he had learned hers. Her eyes and lips and hands explored every inch of his dark masculine body and found him a truly magnificent animal.

When he took her hand and curled it around the part of him most aching for her touch, at first Julianna worried that he'd find her touch awkward and too inexperienced. But soon, her fascination with the differences between the male and female terran body made her forget the last of her Sarnian inhibitions.

His sex, which looked so hard and dangerous, was as smooth as silk. She explored its rigid, dark length at first with her fingertips, then, her lips. When he groaned deep in his throat, a sound that reverberated around the room like the mating growl of a male rock tiger, she experienced a delicious sense of pure feminine power.

Their bodies were damp with perspiration. A musky scent more erotic than the most expensive perfume surrounded them. Julianna gave herself up to her feelings, surrendering eagerly, willingly to Dylan, because he had surrendered so wonderfully to her.

"Dammit, Julianna . . ." Dylan reached for her, but she deftly evaded his vague touch.

A bead of moisture appeared at the end of his shaft, looking like a gleaming pearl on purple satin. When she gathered it in with the tip of her tongue, Dylan's control, which had been slipping away in hot increments, snapped.

He caught her by the waist, then rolled her over onto her back. Trapping her sweet, treacherous hands above her head, he smothered any protest she might try to make with his mouth, tasting himself on her voluptuous lips.

He covered her slick body with his. When he began to penetrate her, she gasped and stiffened.

"Shh," he soothed, brushing her hair away from her face with one hand while his gentle fingers stroked the ultrasensitive little nub of flesh he'd taught her about while they'd been washing each other in the tub. "It'll be okay, sweetheart. Put your legs around me."

"Like this?" She wrapped her long legs around his hips.

"Oh, yes." A long, ragged shudder racked him.

Julianna closed her eyes as his intimate touch began to arouse her all over again. An unfamiliar combination of relaxation and tenseness came over her as she felt her heat becoming wet and slick once more. She arched against his hand, inviting more.

Dylan murmured sweet, encouraging words in her ear, as he very slowly and very tenderly began to enter her, following a pattern of ebbing and flowing, withdrawing each time he felt her tense.

Gradually she softened, opening deeper and deeper as she abandoned herself to these new terrifying, wonderful feelings, and to him.

Finally, with one final deep surge, he plunged all the way into her, breaking through the shield of her virginity, filling her completely.

There was a sharp pain that was swiftly burned away by the pleasurable heat shimmering through Julianna.

"Did I hurt you?"

She was hot and slick and fit him like a glove. Little pulses throbbed deep within her, caressing his aching length like stroking fingers. With every vestige of self-restraint, Dylan remained still, allowing her to adjust to the feel of him inside her.

"Only for a moment." Her legs tightened around him and she pressed closer, her hips moving rhythmically in appeal. "It's getting better."

Hunger was a fist, clenching and clawing and twisting within him. Dylan withdrew ever so slightly, but her hands, free now, clutched at his tight buttocks and pulled him back against her.

"Juls—" he warned on a ragged moan of need.

And then he was moving against her, burying himself in her, forgetting his vow to be gentle, forgetting his promise to take her slowly, forgetting everything but his desperate, driving need. Her nails were digging into his flesh, her teeth nipped at the cord in his neck.

And then his climax was coming—too soon, damn it. He shouted her name. Like a promise. Or a prayer.

And then he collapsed on top of her.

She lay in his arms, warm and trembling, trying to understand her swirling, turmoiled emotions.

Dylan lifted his head, gave her a slanted, slightly rueful smile and brushed some errant strands of damp hair from her cheek. "I'm sorry."

"You don't have to be sorry, Dylan," she said quickly. "I wanted you to make love to me. Very much."

"I was talking about you not being satisfied."

"Satisfied?"

He tried to figure out how to explain climax. "Pleasured."

"But I received a great deal of pleasure," she said with a mixture of earnestness, innocence and absolute honesty he was finding more and more appealing.

He brushed a soft, teasing kiss against her mouth. "It gets better."

"Surely not!" Her disbelief was written all over her exquisite flushed face. But then, remarkably, she felt him growing inside her once again.

"Honest," he promised.

He began to move slowly, tantalizingly, leading her into a new galaxy of high, soaring peaks. Each time she'd go crashing over one jagged peak, he'd take her higher, then higher still, until they'd reached a dazzling place of exploding stars and shooting comets.

And each step of the way, as she pursued the gleaming brilliance, she clung to him, her hands thrust into his jet hair, her long, slender, trembling legs twined tightly around his hips, gasping, moaning, crying out, until she found herself falling, falling, engulfed in a blaze of fiery light.

"That," he said, with obvious satisfaction as he kissed the tears of joy from her flushed face, "was much, much better."

Exhausted, emotionally drained, all she could manage was a soft smile of agreement.

And when he murmured against her lips that he loved her, Julianna, who'd been continually challenging Dylan since his unexpected arrival on Sarnia, didn't argue.

11

"SHOULDN'T YOU START getting ready?" Julianna asked after they'd basked in the warm afterglow of shared passion for a long, comfortable time.

He ran his palm down her back, from her shoulder to her thigh, thinking how her soft skin reminded him of the undersides of the tea roses that grew in his Grandmother Prescott's Castle Mountain garden. If he had his way, Dylan decided, he'd never move from this spot again.

"Get ready for what?"

"For your intended gambling contest." Her tone, so sweet and acquiescent earlier, while they'd been making love, had regained its disapproving edge. But at least she wasn't arguing with him. Dylan decided that, in itself, was a vast improvement.

"Don't worry. I've got loads of time."

"Exactly how much time is a load?"

As a fellow scientist, Dylan understood Julianna's continuous insistence on detail; as her lover, he found her inability to just go with the flow more than a little frustrating.

Skimming his mouth down her throat, he mumbled something inarticulate into the soft skin between shoulder and neck.

Julianna fought against the rising tide of desire created by his intimate kiss. "Would you please repeat that?" she asked on a voice that was huskier than she would have liked. "I couldn't quite hear you."

Dylan's lips were burning a trail down to her breasts. Part of Julianna wanted nothing more than to close her eyes and experience all the glorious, resplendent pleasure this man could bring her.

Another part of her, the part speaking out the loudest at this moment, suspected that he was purposefully using his clever seduction skills in an attempt to sidetrack the conversation.

When he captured one taut, aching nipple between his teeth and nipped gently, Julianna's hands curled into fists, grabbing up handfuls of sheeting.

"Dylan," she protested, "I really would like an answer."

He sighed and lifted his head. "The game's five days away."

"Five days!"

"That's what I said."

"Don't tell me you actually intend for us to stay here for the next five days?"

"That's precisely what I intend."

"Let me get this straight." She sat up, pulling the sheet to cover her breasts. "Against all that is reasonable, you intend to risk our valuable crystals in some ridiculous, illogical game.

"And what is worse, you expect me to remain here in this—" her tawny eyes circled the room with obvious disdain "—place, for five long days while we wait for this event to take place."

Warm feelings lingering from the pure pleasure of making love to Julianna kept Dylan from becoming irritated by either her disparaging tone or her accusation.

"While I'll admit this room—hell, the entire asteroid, for that matter—isn't exactly Shangri-la, yeah, that's it in a nutshell."

"What logical reason could you have for such behavior?"

She wanted to understand. Truly she did. Also, Julianna admitted reluctantly to herself, she needed some proof, however slight, that she had not made the mistake of giving her heart to an entirely different man than she'd believed Dylan to be.

In their brief time together, she'd seen him rise to challenge after challenge with intelligence, ingenuity and remarkable good humor. But now he was displaying a distressing streak of irresponsibility. One that could, considering the price on their heads, end up getting them both killed.

"Simple." He sat up beside her, looped his arm lightly around her shoulder, ignored her sudden stiffening and kissed the top of her now-dry head.

"The bartender told me that five days from now, this place is going to be crawling with transport pilots. And since we need a ship to return to Sarnia, I figured I'd use the crystals as a stake to win us one."

He'd thrown too many startling ideas at her at once. Julianna's mind scrambled to take them one at a time. "You intend to use the crystals to win a ship?"

"Yep."

"You are that certain of your luck?"

"I'm that certain of my skill," he corrected mildly. He didn't add that he'd taught his homemade computer to play poker before his seventh birthday.

"Not knowing either the game, or your skills, first-hand, I shall have to take your word for that," she said. "And if we get this ship, you plan to return to Sarnia?"

"When."

"When, what?"

"You said, *if* I win the ship. I was simply pointing out that the proper word is *when*."

She waved his correction away with an impatient shake of her hand. "Whatever. What I wish to discuss is why you intend to return to Sarnia."

"I thought you wanted to clear your name. And to help the truth get out to the people."

"I do, but—"

"Then that's what we're going to do."

"*We?* As in you and I?"

"See anyone else in this room?"

"No, but—"

"Then, yeah, I guess that leaves *we* as in you and I."

"You will be risking your life."

Dylan shrugged. "It won't be the first time since landing in your world."

"But why would you do that? For me?"

"Simple." He took her hand and laced their fingers together. "I love you."

"That is impossible," she protested, even as she desperately wanted it to be true.

Dylan lifted a brow. "Are you suggesting that you're unlovable?"

Julianna wished that he wouldn't tease her about such an important subject. "I am merely pointing out that it is highly illogical to fall in love with someone you do not know."

"After what we've just shared, I think we know each other pretty well, Juls." He lifted their joined hands to his lips and kissed her knuckles.

"Although you're probably right about love being illogical," he decided. "But just because something's illogical, doesn't mean that it can't exist." Unfolding her fingers, he pressed a kiss against the inside of her palm before nibbling at the sensitive flesh at the base of her thumb.

Her mind was whirling, trying to take in his words while his mouth was creating havoc within her body.

"What do you intend to do when we get to Sarnia?"

He watched the heat rise in her cheeks and decided that he'd never felt less like talking. "I don't have all the details worked out yet," he admitted. "But you'll be the first to know when I've come up with a plan."

"How encouraging," she said on a dry tone that she was a very long way from feeling. In truth, it was happening all over again. His heat was seeping into her, making her burn. "And how do you suggest we spend the next five days?"

"That's an easy one." He pulled her down beside him, his hands reclaiming her. "I figured we'd spend it getting to know one another better."

Once again, against her better judgment, despite the fact that she had been captain of the debate team during her student years at the Science Institute, Julianna could think of not one single logical argument.

OVER THE NEXT FIVE DAYS, Julianna and Dylan hardly left the room. And during their secluded, intimate time together, they did, indeed, come to know each other well. And not just in the physical sense, although they did manage to make love more times, and in more ways, than Julianna ever would have imagined possible.

However, since even they couldn't make love all the time, they spent many long hours talking, about everything and nothing.

Dylan learned that Julianna had always felt as if she were growing up in Starbuck's shadow. And although she was the first to admit that her parents had gone out of their way to treat their children as equals, she'd felt dwarfed by her brother's brilliance.

"Although Starbuck assured me, and I've seen for myself, that you're pretty brilliant, yourself, sweetheart," Dylan said, "I suppose that explains why you worked overtime to become such a proper little Sarnian."

Once, Julianna might have been surprised by his insight. No longer. "Self-restraint was the one thing that always gave Starbuck great difficulty," she agreed. "It was easier for me."

Because it had been too long since he'd kissed her—at least five minutes—Dylan gathered her hair into a knot at the back of her neck and drew her to him for a long, lingering time.

"Yeah," he teased a great deal later, "you're a wonder of self-restraint."

"I always was," she insisted. "Until you."

He gave her a look rife with sensual memories and erotic promises. "Believe me, Juls, I know the feeling. Very well."

"I don't understand why I feel this way whenever I am with you," she admitted softly.

"Simple." He linked their fingers together, lifted their hands and kissed her fingertips. "You're a scientist, Juls. Surely you've studied chemistry at that famous Science Institute."

"Of course. But there is one thing my illustrious professors failed to teach me."

His lips moved to the tender flesh at her palm. "What's that?"

Julianna felt herself melting yet again. "That chemistry could be so much fun," she managed.

While Dylan was learning about Julianna, she was discovering things about him, and his life, as well.

She learned he'd admired his father—Castle Mountain's former police chief—more than any man he'd ever met. He spoke of both his grief for his father's death and his love for his mother with an unself-conscious openness that no Sarnian man would have ever exhibited.

And she couldn't help noticing that his eyes, when he spoke of his sister Charity, turned warm with absolute affection. He was a man who obviously loved his family a great deal.

Which was why, Julianna reminded herself firmly, he would soon be returning to his own planet and his own time. And although even days ago she would have found the idea an anathema, Julianna now found herself almost hoping that when Dylan did leave, he'd ask her to go with him.

"She sounds very loving," Julianna said, after Dylan had described the way his sister had of constantly rescuing stray animals. Although keeping pets had long been declared illogical on Sarnia, Julianna admired Charity's obviously caring nature.

"She is that. After college, she went to law school because she wanted to help the underprivileged. But she's far from perfect. In fact, not only is she as stubborn as another lovely lady I know, unfortunately, she also has a helluva impatient streak."

"Like Starbuck," Julianna murmured.

"Exactly." Dylan grinned. "Anyway, to make a long story short, the system moved too slowly for her, so she decided she could help people more by putting the bad guys behind bars where they couldn't hurt anyone. Even after years of dealing with criminals, she still manages to see good in almost everything," Dylan said. "And everyone."

"It sounds as if my brother is a lucky man."

"Nearly as lucky as me," he agreed.

Thinking of the life his sister and Starbuck were embarking upon, Dylan found himself, not for the first time, wanting to ask Julianna to return to Earth with him.

But knowing how she felt about truth and honor, he'd decided not to push her into a decision she was not prepared to make. Especially since they'd gone a remarkable four and a half days without a single argument.

Although she'd read hundreds, thousands, of documents depicting terran life in the past, Julianna learned more about Earth and its inhabitants from this halcyon time with Dylan than from any dry history texts.

In turn, Julianna tried to fill Dylan in on her own time, answering every one of his many questions as best she could, although when it came to his scientific inquiries, she was often forced to tell him that he'd simply have to ask Starbuck. After he arrived back on his own planet. And his own time. Even as she knew Dylan must return to Earth, she found herself dreading that time more with each passing day.

And then the day of the game was here.

"I suppose you're going to insist I remain in the room," she said as he dressed for the game.

"Actually, I was hoping you'd join me. For luck."

Having tried to guard her unruly heart against caring too much for a man who would soon be out of her life, Julianna was appalled at exactly how much pleasure she received from that simple invitation.

"I thought you didn't need luck."

"A good-luck charm never hurts," he said easily. His warm blue eyes moved over her face, her tousled silver hair, her bare shoulders. "And you're the most charming good-luck piece I've ever seen."

"That's incredibly chauvinistic," she felt obliged to point out. "But it's also very nice."

"It's the truth." He tossed her the gilt dress she'd been wearing when they'd first arrived at the outpost. "But you'd better get dressed, because if any of those transport pirates saw you the way you look right now, we'd have a full-scale riot on our hands."

Julianna saw the flash of heat in his eyes as his gaze roved slowly over her, and told herself that a compliment based on her physical attributes, rather than her mind, should not bring her so much heady pleasure.

It should not.

But it did.

HOURS LATER, they were still downstairs at the gambling tables. Although Julianna had to admit that Dylan was as good a cardplayer as he'd claimed, she couldn't help the frisson of fear that skimmed up her spine every time she watched him reach into the leather bag, pull out yet another crystal and toss it into the center of the table.

He'd explained the rules of the game upstairs, going over the system of raises, folds, calls and bets so she would better understand what was going on.

Watching him play, it did not take her long to realize that he was keeping track of the cards in order to calculate his odds of winning each hand. It was, she decided, something Starbuck would have done.

Once again Julianna considered how very alike both men were. And for the first time, she admitted, albeit only to herself, that she loved them both.

A low murmur around the table returned her attention to the card game. Dylan had just discarded all his cards and was drawing again. It was not the first time he'd done such a thing.

And although he'd told her that he never settled for a small win if the cards offered any chance for the big win, such seemingly reckless abandon made her pulse hammer faster.

Earlier all the tables in the room were filled with gamblers. Finally, as more and more players dropped out, all the action moved to one center table, where only seven grim-faced terran transport pilots and Dylan were still competing.

The day wore on. The acrid air in the room, from the fat, black cigars favored by the pilots, became as thick and stifling as the smoke from the still-active volcanoes on the planet Pelenian.

Gradually the other players folded, as well, leaving Dylan in a face-to-face encounter with the roughest looking of the terran pilots. When Julianna had first caught sight of the raised red scar running down the side of the pilot's granitelike face, she'd known that this was a man who'd endured and inflicted more than his share of violence.

As the cards were dealt, Julianna wished that Dylan would just take his winnings and leave. Now, while he was still alive. But she knew he wouldn't. Not until he'd stripped the pilot of everything but his beloved ship. And then, heaven help him, he intended to go for that, too.

The pile of stones in front of Dylan continued to grow while the stack in front of the pilot diminished.

Finally, amazingly, just as Dylan had predicted, the two men were playing, double or nothing, the crystals for the transport pilot's sleek, dark smuggling ship.

Standing over Dylan's shoulder, Julianna schooled her expression to one of absolute calm when she viewed the miserable cards he'd been dealt. She hoped her face did not reveal the discouragement she felt.

To her dismay, he held, turning down the opportunity to discard and draw new cards. The pilot stared at his cards, then at Dylan's face—and Julianna's—then back at his cards. Although he was not nearly as intelligent as Dylan, he'd proven himself an expert gambler.

Finally, after contemplating Dylan's raise for a long, silent time, he cursed, then threw his cards into the center of the table.

It had been a bluff, Julianna realized as Dylan scooped up the electronic ignition starter. A daring, illogical, wonderful bluff. She experienced a surge of womanly pride in Dylan's daring. Then Julianna viewed the smuggler's face and imagined she could see the steam coming from his ears.

"Thanks for the game, guys," Dylan said. "And now, as much as we'd like to stick around, I think my wife and I will inspect our new ship."

"How about a drink first?" the disgruntled pilot asked.

Dylan's smile was wide and ingratiating. "Sounds terrific," he agreed. "After we inspect the ship." And then, he managed to surprise Julianna yet again. "Would you like to come with us?" he asked. "To give us the grand tour?"

The pilot's stony face relaxed and Julianna didn't need Starbuck's mind-reading ability to know what he was thinking. That he had no intention of allowing Julianna and Dylan to leave was obvious.

Wondering how Dylan intended to get around that dilemma, she followed the two men out the door and down the dusty street, relieved when the other pilots seemed content to stay inside the cool dark room and resume drinking their flagons of Enos Ale.

The ship was smaller than the prison ship, built for speed and scanner avoidance. The pilot's pride in his ship was evident, and for a brief moment Julianna allowed herself a moment's pity about taking it.

But then he began to brag of all the laws he'd broken, describing a few of his more colorful crimes, including several cold-blooded murders, and her sympathy disintegrated.

After examining the operating system, Dylan shot Julianna a quick look that told her it was time to go. But there was no way they could take off with this renegade still on board. So, deciding that when something worked, she should stick with it, Julianna pulled out the act she'd worked on the guard back on the *Mutiny*.

While Dylan studied the remote guidance system, Julianna wandered toward the cramped living quarters. The dark metal wall was covered with posters of provocatively posed terran and Cyprian nude females.

"You must be very brave," she said, slanting the rogue pilot a warm smile brimming over with feminine admiration. "To have had so many death-defying adventures."

The pilot shrugged. "It comes with the territory."

"Granted." She moved a little closer and licked her lips. "But how many men, I wonder, would have the nerve to do the things you've done?" Her gaze trapped his. "Are you so daring in everything you do?"

The invitation was there, sparkling in her eyes, hovering on her wet lips, lingering in the touch of her hand on his arm.

"You get rid of lover boy," the pilot growled, "and I'll show you."

His rough, wide hand settled intimately on her hip. "That's a very intriguing invitation," she allowed.

On cue, Dylan's fist came out of the shadows, striking the pilot's jaw. "Unfortunately," Julianna continued as the man slumped down the wall and crumpled to the floor, "I think I shall have to turn it down."

"You're getting better," Dylan said as he dragged the unconscious pilot to the open doorway. From his tone, Julianna had the feeling he didn't exactly mean it as a compliment.

"I suppose that's one of the problems with making love to a virgin," she said calmly. "Once he introduces a woman to the pleasures of lovemaking, a man must undoubtedly worry that she'll begin to wonder how such an act would be with someone else."

Her words hit just a little too close to home. "You thinking of doing a little experimenting, Juls?" The primal male jealousy curling through his gut had Dylan tossing the pilot out onto the tarmac with more force than necessary.

"No."

It was only a single word, not a declaration of undying love. But it spoke volumes. Dylan stood in the doorway, hands on his hips, looked into her face and knew exactly how Starbuck had felt when he'd chosen to remain on Earth.

"Good," he answered. "Now you'd better sit down and fasten your seat belt. I don't want to be still hanging around here when that guy wakes up. Or his cronies discover what happened to him."

As Julianna took her place in the copilot's seat, Dylan closed the door, employed the air lock, then, with a rapid-fire movement over the computer keypad, started the ship.

It rose straight up, breaking through the reins of gravity like a rocket.

"Dylan?" Julianna said softly, once the ship was on course, speeding its way toward Sarnia.

"Yeah, Juls?" His attention was directed toward the computer screen.

"I love you." There, she'd said it. And, amazingly, the world hadn't started spinning out of control. In fact, the declaration had proven remarkably freeing.

"I know." Dylan typed in additional coordinates.

"You know?" Julianna stared at him. She didn't know what, exactly, she'd expected, but she certainly hadn't expected him to be so blasé about a monumental confession she'd never, ever, intended to make to any man. "That's all you have to say?"

He glanced up at the computer, grinned, curled his hand around her neck and pulled her to him for a short, hard kiss that left her breathless.

"It certainly took you long enough to admit it."

"Love is an alien concept on Sarnia. I wanted to be certain," Julianna said softly.

His palm cupped her cheek. "And are you?"

Her eyes met his. "I am more sure of loving you than I have ever been of anything in my life."

Dylan exhaled a long breath he had not been aware of holding. "That being the case, I suppose I'd better figure out a way to keep you alive awhile longer."

She'd come to understand that just as she'd worked so hard to conceal her innermost feelings, Dylan's teasing was often his way of handling his own tumultuous emotions. That being the case, she did not take offense at his lighthearted attitude to such a serious problem.

Instead, she put aside her regrets that they could not dwell on these feelings of love a little longer. After all, she assured herself, there would be time for that once they'd salvaged her reputation, restored her family's good name, had her conviction overturned and saved her life.

Some individuals might find such goals impossible. But Julianna had absolute faith in their succeeding. Together she and Dylan had already accomplished the improbable.

The impossible would just take a little longer.

12

THE PLAN TO VINDICATE Julianna and win her pardon was basically a simple, albeit dangerous, one. Once they arrived in Sarnia's orbit, they would slip between the scanners, following in the shadow of one of the large commercial ships that constantly entered and departed the planet, allowing them to land beneath the planet dome.

Then they would go to Rachel Valderian's house, where Julianna would remain while Dylan retrieved the letters and journals Julianna had hidden away.

After retrieving her proof, he would then take them back to the house, showing them to the gathering of trusted Elders Rachel would call together.

Next, hopefully the men in question would live up to their renowned integrity and submit the evidence to the Ruling Council, which, when faced with the irrefutable truth, would have no other choice but to reverse Julianna's conviction.

The true story of how the government had come to be established would be painful for the citizens of Sarnia to accept. But, Dylan assured Julianna, eventually, everyone would adjust. It certainly wouldn't be the first time a government admitted to having made a major miscalculation.

As they approached her home planet, Julianna could only hope that Dylan was right.

A huge government transport plane was nearing the access to the dome. With a deft skill Julianna admired, Dylan brought the small sleek ship tight beneath the plane's wide belly, ignoring the warning complaint from the on-board computer that he was cutting the distance between this ship and the enormous vessel too close.

"What the hell?" he muttered as he gazed down at the scene below.

Unbelievably, for a planet famous throughout the galaxy for its serenity, chaos ruled. The streets were clogged with people running in all directions.

As the ground grew closer, Dylan could see the expression on the inhabitants' faces. To a person, it was stark, primal fear. Seeking information, he scanned through the radio signals, receiving only static.

"Don't tell me this three-ring circus is typical Truth fest behavior."

"No," Julianna murmured, her own eyes unable to take in such an unfamiliar sight. "This is totally uncharacteristic. I have never seen anything like it."

She watched, appalled, as a man, racing across the street, literally ran over a young woman. Screeching something in response, the woman struggled to her feet, her arms and legs badly skinned and bleeding.

At the last minute, Dylan pulled out from beneath the larger ship, landing the small craft on the tarmac nearby. His earlier worry about managing to arrive undetected had proven groundless, he realized. Everyone was too caught up in their own panic to notice one lone transport vehicle.

He helped Julianna down from the ship, then reached out and snagged the arm of a passerby. "What's going on?"

"You don't know?" The man's face was as white as chalk, his eyes wide with terror.

"If we knew we wouldn't be asking," Julianna pointed out with the Sarnian logic that Dylan knew was as much her birthright as her very human emotions.

"A monstrous meteor is headed toward Sarnia," the man revealed. "Large enough, astrophysicists say, to destroy the entire planet."

"That meteor was destroyed during the last solar revolution," Julianna protested, remembering the occasion well.

Once Sarnian astrophysicists had spotted its approach, the government had blasted it with laser beams, effectively changing its trajectory.

"The Elders were wrong," the man said. "Or else they lied. Perhaps it changed course suddenly. Whatever happened, newscom reported that it is due to strike at any time. Everyone must evacuate! Immediately!"

With that he shook off Dylan's hand and took off running again.

Dylan and Julianna exchanged a look. A cry of fear and despair escaped her throat. "My mother—"

"We'll save her," Dylan broke in quickly. Confidently. "Don't worry, sweetheart, we've enough crystals for all three of us to get to Earth."

This time, Julianna did not argue. It had been enough that Dylan had been willing to return to Sarnia with her. Now it appeared that soon her home planet would cease to exist.

Julianna knew the pain of that unpalatable truth would sink in. Later. At the moment, all her thoughts were focused on reaching her mother. And escaping this nightmare.

Hand in hand, Julianna and Dylan struggled against a tide of frantic Sarnians all seeming to be going in the opposite direction. People were screaming, crushing one another in an attempt to climb aboard the various aircraft crowding the tarmac.

"Whatever happened to orderly evacuation plans?" Dylan had to shout to be heard over the cries and screams.

"The threat of impending death tends to override logic," Julianna shouted back, remembering her own cold fear as she'd waited for her executioner to arrive.

But Dylan had shown up instead and her life had inexorably changed.

Desperate to know that her mother was safe, Julianna struggled through the crowd, shoving and punching those around her in a way she never could have less than two weeks ago.

Men and women were shouting; children were crying. There was violence in the streets and widespread looting as people attempted to gather valuables to trade for essentials on other planets.

By the time they reached her mother's house, Julianna's insides were knotted with fear. When she discovered the servants gone, the house ransacked, and her mother was missing, she felt the blood drain from her face.

"You're not going to faint." Dylan's strong fingers curved around her shoulders and he shook her, gently but firmly. "It's going to be okay. Your mother's going to be okay."

His handsome face was swimming inches from hers. Julianna blinked, struggling to clear her head.

He retrieved an overturned chair and coaxed her into it just as she thought for certain that her rubbery legs were going to collapse.

"Put your head between your knees. It'll help."

Although Julianna didn't believe anything could help overcome the vertigo that had her in its grip, Dylan didn't give her any choice. He put his hand on the top of her head and pushed downward.

Remarkably Julianna could feel her head clearing, as if she'd been given a whiff of straight paradoxygen.

"Now, think," he said. "Where would she go?"

"To my father's crypt," Julianna answered. "She would never leave without saying goodbye."

"Is it far?" Dylan wasn't at all eager to rejoin the teeming mob filling the streets.

"It's right behind the house. In my mother's garden."

"Bingo." He squatted down beside her. "Are you all right?"

"I'm fine."

"Because, if you'd like to stay here while I go look—"

"No. I'm coming with you."

The crypt had been created from some sort of space-age rocklike material that remarkably resembled marble. Names of generations of Valderians had been etched onto metal plaques lining the walls.

They found Rachel Valderian seated in front of the plaque bearing her late husband's name, her hands folded, her eyes closed, an amazing expression of peace on her still beautiful features.

"Oh, Mother," Julianna breathed gratefully, "thank God."

Rachel's eyes, which were, Dylan noted, a rich tawny hue like her daughter's, opened wide with surprise. "Julianna?" She glanced around. "This doesn't appear to be heaven."

Although the official Sarnian doctrine scoffed at offworld religions, Julianna knew that her mother had absolutely refused to suspend her own beliefs upon marriage to a Sarnian Elder.

"It's not, Mother."

A smile bloomed on Rachel's face. "Then you're really alive."

"Yes." An identical smile curved Julianna's lips. "Thanks to Dylan."

Despite the gravity of their situation, Rachel gave Dylan a very thorough, very motherly once-over. "You're terran."

"I'm from Earth, yes. My name is Dylan Prescott and Starbuck sent me."

"Starbuck?" she demanded. "You must tell me everything!"

"They'll be plenty of time for that, later, Mother," Julianna said. "After we leave."

"Leave? But I'm not going anywhere, darling."

"Mrs. Valderian," Dylan said gently, "perhaps you don't realize what's about to happen."

"A meteor is going to strike Sarnia. It will most likely destroy the planet."

"That's why we have to get away, Mother," Julianna stressed. "Now."

Displaying a stubbornness Dylan had witnessed in both Rachel Valderian's adult children, she shook her head. "You must understand, Julianna, I have made peace with both my maker and my fate. I am prepared to die. Here, with my husband."

"Mother!" Julianna shot Dylan a panicky look. *Do something!* it said.

"That's a very noble intention, Mrs. Valderian," he said gently. "But the days of widows throwing themselves on their husband's funeral pyres are long past.

"I understand why you might have felt this way earlier, when you thought you'd lost your entire family. But, as you can see, Julianna is quite alive. As is Starbuck."

He went for the close. "And if you don't return to Earth with us, you'll miss your son's wedding."

"Starbuck's getting married?"

"To my sister. They intend to make their home on Earth. In Maine."

Rachel appeared to be considering that. "I've always liked Maine," she said, rising to her feet.

"Does that mean you'll come with us?" Julianna asked.

Rachel turned toward the crypt, running her fingers over the block letters spelling out her husband's name.

"If you'll just leave me alone with your father for a moment, Julianna, I'll be right with you."

Relief was instantaneous. Julianna burst into unashamed tears of joy.

ALTHOUGH THEY'D MANAGED to overcome one more important hurdle, Dylan couldn't allow himself to relax. There was still the little matter of getting to Starbuck's laboratory, where they could use the computers, the power boosted by the electrical charge of the crystals, to beam them through time and space to Castle Mountain.

Fortunately, this time, the tide of people was with them, and although it was still far from easygoing, they managed to reach the lab.

After giving Dylan the computer program her brother had used to travel to Earth in the first place, Julianna joined her mother across the room. There, she did her best to fill her mother in on all the changes in Starbuck's life.

"That is the man who helped you escape, isn't it?" Rachel asked when Julianna had told her everything she knew about her brother's adventure.

"It's a long, complicated story. But yes. Dylan saved my life."

"And now, against all logic, you have fallen in love with him."

Julianna felt herself blushing. "Is it that obvious?"

"Yes. And you've no idea how pleased I am. How pleased your father would be."

"Father?" Julianna was certain she must have mis-understood. "Surely Father would have preferred I bond with a proper Sarnian."

Rachel surprised her by laughing at that. The soft, silvery sound drew Dylan's momentary attention and earned his smile before he returned to work at the computer.

"Darling, wherever did you get an idea like that?"

"I just assumed . . ." Julianna's voice drifted off.

"When I met your father, he was the youngest ambassador to Earth in the history of Sarnia," Rachel said. "I was three years out of college and working as an undersecretary of protocol at the United States White House. I was assigned to pick Xanthus up at the space-port. The moment I saw him, looking so tall and dark and handsome and distinguished, I fell head over heels in love."

Julianna remembered all too well the unsettling emotions she'd experienced when Dylan showed up at her door. "The same thing happened to me," she mur-mured. "But I didn't realize it."

"Of course you wouldn't," Rachel agreed. "Because you've had a proper Sarnian upbringing. Which was essential for a member of the ruling family. Your father didn't recognize his feelings at first, either."

A soft, reminiscent smile curved her lips. "He later told me that he'd thought it was the unfamiliar, spicy terran food that had kept him awake all night."

"But it was you."

Rachel nodded. "Xanthus had fallen in love as well. But duty had been ingrained in him since childhood and he had difficulty breaking such a long-lasting taboo of descendants of the Ancient Ones entering into mixed marriages. Besides, which, he was already bonded to the daughter of his father's best friend.

"Since neither of us wanted to hurt an innocent person, we tried our best to stay apart. But our work kept putting us together, and finally, late one night—it was during the Christmas holiday season—after an embassy ball, we made love. And it was absolutely wonderful."

Despite the past days with Dylan, or perhaps because of them, Julianna was more than a little uncomfortable hearing about her parents' lovemaking. But, lost in her own romantic reverie, Rachel appeared not to notice.

"During his first year at the embassy, although we thought we were being discreet, now that I look back on it, I realize that love is one emotion a person cannot conceal."

"What happened?" Julianna had always suspected, more from what her parents hadn't said, than what they had, that their romance had not exactly been a smooth one.

"Your father was recalled by the Ruling Council, which put pressure on him to break our affair off."

"But he didn't."

"He refused," Rachel agreed. "But when he didn't immediately return to Earth, I began to worry. I sent several messages to him, but received no answer. After a month had passed without any word from Xanthus, I screwed up my courage and went to the embassy and asked the chargé d'affaires if he was all right.

"That's when I was told that he had resigned his post as ambassador in order to take a job working as an aide to the chief justice of the Sarnian court."

A shadow moved across her eyes at the long-ago memory. "For the first seven days after hearing that news, I thought my heart was going to break." Even now, years later, the pain of that lonely week made her eyes glisten suspiciously.

Caught up in the story, and her mother's reaction to it, Julianna forgot all about the rioting outside the building, and more remarkably, what Dylan was currently doing across the room.

"And on the eighth day?" she prompted gently.

Rachel shook herself slightly, as if trying to shake off the distant pain. "I resigned my own post at the White House, cashed in all my savings, sold my apartment, gave my cat to my best friend at the protocol department and bought a ticket on the first transport ship going to Sarnia."

"You actually chased after my father?" As uninhibited as Dylan had taught her to be, at least in bed, Julianna could not imagine such rash behavior.

"I loved him," Rachel answered simply. "As you love Dylan."

As Julianna looked at Dylan, a warm feeling flowed through her and she understood all too well her mother's behavior.

"Father must have been surprised when you showed up so unexpectedly," she guessed.

Rachel laughed. "'Surprised' doesn't begin to cover it. What I'd had no way of knowing was that his own father had become ill, forcing Xanthus to remain on Sarnia until the danger had passed.

"He'd sent word to me through the embassy, explaining everything, but his letters were mysteriously lost."

"The same way yours had disappeared," Julianna guessed.

"Exactly. As it turned out, your poor father was having a much worse time than I. . . .

"Not only had he been forced to face the disapproval of the Ruling Council, not to mention the icy fury of his former bondmate, but his father had been on the verge of death and on top of that, when I failed to respond to all his messages, he'd thought I'd changed my mind about my feelings for him. Which, of course, couldn't have been further from the truth.

"We were married as soon as his father recovered. Nine months later, Starbuck was born. Then, four years after that, we had you. And for thirty years I doubt you could have found a happier couple anywhere in either galaxy."

Julianna had to ask. "Despite the differences between you?"

Rachel's gaze went from her daughter's face to Dylan, then back again. "I'm not going to deny that there weren't problems, Julianna. But all couples have some difficulty adjusting to marriage. I always thought, and your father agreed, that our differences balanced out nicely."

She patted her daughter's hand reassuringly. "Surely, in your studies, you've read of yin and yang."

"The terran Chinese philosophy declaring that the interaction between two principles—yin being negative, dark and feminine, and yang being positive, bright and male—influences the destinies of all creatures and things?"

"I knew you were a clever girl," Rachel said approvingly. "That's how your father and I viewed ourselves. And, from what you've told me about Starbuck and Charity Prescott, I suspect that their differences are also their strength."

"Dylan said they believe that destiny brought them together," Julianna allowed. At the time, she hadn't believed in destiny. Or fate. But that was in the days she would always consider B.D. Before Dylan.

"I suspect fate did play a role. And in turn, Starbuck landing in the wrong place at the wrong time was ultimately responsible for Dylan coming to Sarnia. Destiny," Rachel affirmed, "is a mystifying, marvelous thing."

"It's also a little frightening."

"Only if you allow it to be. And I don't recall rearing a coward for a daughter."

Julianna's worried gaze returned to Dylan, and like vapor, the last of her fears and worries disintegrated.

Giving her mother a kiss on the cheek, she rose and walked across the room to join the man she loved.

When he felt her hand on his shoulder, Dylan glanced up and smiled. "Almost done."

"You are sure it will work?"

"As sure as I can be."

"That is enough for me."

He laughed at that. A rich, deep rumbling sound Julianna knew would still thrill her when she was eighty.

"Such confidence from a woman who once doubted my every word?"

"I doubt nothing about you, Dylan Prescott."

"Not even my illogical, irrational love?"

Her answering smile was every bit as warm as his laugh. "Especially not that."

The computer, scanning its way through the Milky Way galaxy, suddenly beeped as the blue, cloud-shrouded sphere that was Earth appeared on the screen. And then the scene moved nearer, appearing the way it might through ever-increasing intensities of a telescopic lens, through the clouds, over vast green oceans and jagged snow-clad mountains, to first North America, then the state of Maine, ending finally, at Charity Prescott's door in Castle Mountain, Maine.

"Ready?" Dylan asked.

Julianna drew in a deep breath. "Ready."

"Mrs. Valderian?"

"Please, call me Rachel," the older woman said as she joined them. "And yes, I suppose I'm as ready as I'll ever be."

"We'll send your mother first," Dylan decided. Since the computer would need reprompting for each traveler, he would be the last to leave Sarnia.

As Julianna embraced her mother, hot tears stung at the back of her eyelids. "Have a safe trip," she said, in much the same way she might if her mother were merely taking a slight jaunt across the domed planet to visit friends.

"Don't worry." Rachel's expression was as serene as that of a Sarnian Elder. "We'll all be sitting around the table eating Maine lobster before you know it." She took the crystal Dylan handed her, walked into the imaging circle, turned to him and said, "Let's get this show on the road."

"You're a brave woman, Mrs., uh, Rachel," Dylan corrected.

"Hogwash. I'm not at all brave." Julianna's mother surprised him with a bold wink. "I simply have no intention of passing up a chance to be a grandmother."

With that she was gone, disappearing from the room in a scattering of golden sparkles.

"Well." Dylan let out his breath. "She's on her way."

"Yes." Julianna looked at the circle where her mother had been standing only moments before, then down at the screen.

Was she already there? On that whirling blue globe? Was she already having a joyous reunion with the son she'd thought she'd lost?

"Well," Julianna said, "I suppose I'm next."

"That's the plan." Dylan rose, laced their hands together and walked with her to the imaging circle. "We're going to make it," he said, his gaze as sober as she'd ever seen it. "You and I and your mom, we're all going to be in Castle Mountain before we know it.

"And after we arrive, I have every intention of marrying you. Despite any arguments you might be able to think up against the idea."

Loving him more than she'd ever believed it possible to love anyone, Julianna flung her arms around his neck. "I thought you'd never ask," she said on a mixture of laughter and tears.

His head swooped down and his lips covered hers and they were kissing. Heat flowed out of Dylan and into Julianna; joy shimmered out of her and into him. Their arms, their minds, their hearts tangled, and for a suspended time there was no past, no future, only this glorious present.

Then the building shook. Once. Twice. Again. When the windows began to shatter, flying outward, both knew that it was not their shared kiss that had caused the world to rock.

"The meteor," Julianna gasped. "It's hit."

"If that had happened, I doubt this place would still be standing," Dylan corrected. "I think it's just fragments. For now."

His arms tightened around her, as if he could keep her safe by the sheer strength of his not-inconsiderable will. A series of explosions outside rocked the building again. The overhead halozite lights crackled, sparks flew all around them.

"You've got to leave, sweetheart. Now."

Outside the blown-out windows, the planet was on fire. Julianna could smell the smoke, hear the terrorized screams of her fellow Sarnians.

"I can't leave you. Not like this."

"Damn it, Juls, you're leaving." He pressed the sparkling blue stone into her hand and closed her fingers around it. "Now."

Dylan gave her one last hard, breath-stealing kiss, then before she could move from the circle, he raced back to the computer, pushed the transporter button and watched the woman he loved disintegrate.

An errant spark from the overhead lights had landed on a stack of computer paper. The paper, made from a chemical compound rather than the amalgam of wood and cloth Dylan was accustomed to on Earth, immediately went up in a flash of blue flames.

Dylan said a quick, heartfelt prayer, reset the computer, pushed a delayed release button, then stood in the exact same spot he'd last seen Julianna and Rachel.

As he, too, left Starbuck's laboratory, Sarnia exploded in a blinding white fireball.

And then there was nothing. Only cold black space.

13

IT WAS A WHITE CHRISTMAS in Maine.

A group of carolers, clad in nineteenth-century period costumes were singing in the hallways of the Castle Mountain hospital. The pungent scent of the towering fir tree, ablaze with white lights in the lobby and the cozy aroma of gingerbread drifting upstairs from the kitchen overcame the usual medicinal odor of disinfectant.

In Room 206 of the maternity ward, Charity Valderian was holding court. Beside her bed stood her husband, Starbuck, who still looked a little pale from the recent experience, and next to him was Charity's mother, who'd arrived from Wyoming, dressed in faded denim and a blue-checked snap front shirt. Accompanying her was Holt Langely, her new beau, a silver-haired rancher who was wearing his heart on his denim sleeve.

At first Charity had found it strange, seeing her mother with a man other than her father. But since she desperately wanted her mother to be happy, Charity had welcomed him warmly into the family.

In her arms she was holding the guest of honor at this family celebration. Prescott Dylan Valderian had come into the world, howling his dark head off, at precisely one minute after midnight this Christmas morning.

"He's beautiful," Rachel Valderian, standing on the other side of the bed decreed. She'd been living in Castle Mountain for the past nine months, arriving just in time for Charity and Starbuck's wedding and had come to love her daughter-in-law.

"Is he supposed to look like a prune?" Dylan asked. His dark blue eyes swept over the baby's wrinkled red features with an unclelike pride that was at direct odds with his teasing words.

"Dylan!" Julianna said swiftly, giving him a playful slap on the arm. "Prescott does not look like a prune. Apologize to your sister, right now!"

Having discovered long ago in another world and another time that he could not deny this woman anything, Dylan grinned, held up his hands in a gesture of self-defense and said, "Sorry, Charity. Starbuck. Just kidding."

"If I hadn't known that, you would not still be standing," Starbuck said mildly. Remembering his brother-in-law and partner's ancient martial arts skills, Dylan knew that comment, like most of Starbuck's statements, was the absolute truth.

"Well, I think he's perfect," Julianna said, a little wistfully. When Charity had allowed her to hold the baby boy earlier, she'd found herself reluctant to return the infant to his mother.

Although both her brother and Dylan had invited her to come to work with them at the lab, independent as always, she'd chosen her own path. Realizing that her work in xenoanthropology gave her an insider's view of what was still an unknown universe on Earth, she'd written a novel based on her adventure with Dylan.

The manuscript had recently sold to a New York publishing house specializing in science fiction and fantasy. Encouraged, Julianna was currently working on a second book telling the true story about her planet from the diaries she'd brought back with her. Ironically, she'd finally be revealing the truth in the form of commercial fiction.

There was a discreet pop as Dylan opened the champagne he and Julianna had smuggled into the hospital. He poured the sparkling liquid into glasses and handed one to each member of the family.

"To Charity and Starbuck," he said, lifting his glass in a toast. "And to baby Prescott, the best of two worlds."

Everyone drank to the toast. Everyone, Dylan noticed, except Julianna.

"Something wrong?" From her first taste, when Starbuck had brought out the bubbly to celebrate the arrival of his mother, sister and best friend on Earth, Julianna had professed to enjoy champagne.

"Nothing at all." She smiled at him over the rim of her glass. "I just plan to practice some cautious abstinence." Her slow smile widened, filled with secrets, reminding Dylan of a Cheshire cat. "And although I truly hate to steal any lightning from Charity on her special day—"

"Thunder," Starbuck interrupted.

"What?"

"The word is *thunder*. Not lightning. You need to work on your idioms, Julianna," he said helpfully.

"Thank you, brother dear. I will keep that in mind," Julianna agreed calmly.

"Could you just skip the grammar lesson and let her finish," Dylan demanded hotly, turning on his best friend.

Since Julianna knew that the only time Dylan lost his temper was when he was worried about her, she decided not to draw out his agony.

"I merely want to make an announcement."

"I knew it!" Charity said, clapping her hands and exchanging an I-told-you-so look with her husband.

"Damn it," Dylan growled. "Would everyone just be quiet for a minute. My wife is trying to tell me something."

The thought of this beautiful, intelligent, passionate and, yes, challenging woman as his wife thrilled him, just as it had been doing for the six months since their marriage.

"If you're going to be a father, darling," Julianna said with her innate calm, "you are going to have to learn to watch your language. Unless you want our child talking like a lumberjack."

"Of course I don't...." Dylan's voice dropped off and he stared at her as comprehension finally sank in. "Child?" His startled gaze dropped to her still-flat stomach, covered by the beaded red angora Christmas sweater he'd given her last night. "Are you saying—"

"You are going to be a father," Julianna confirmed his unspoken question.

"Look at him!" Charity crowed. "He's a stunned as you were, Starbuck. What is it about brilliant men," she asked, "that they know what's happening all the way across the universe, but can't see what's happening right in front of their noses?"

"A child?"

Julianna saw the pride and joy in Dylan's loving gaze and felt her own eyes grow moist with human emotion. She nodded.

His gaze returned to her stomach, as if imagining it rounded with his child. Their child. "When?"

"July Fourth." She laughed merrily as Dylan pulled her into his arms. Julianna found his touch amusingly tentative, as if she'd suddenly turned to delicate crystal and he was afraid of hurting her. "Isn't that an absolutely perfect, logical day for our all-American baby to be born?"

With the agreement of the others ringing in her ears, Julianna lifted her smiling face for her husband's kiss.

 HARLEQUIN®

THE TAGGARTS OF TEXAS!

Harlequin's Ruth Jean Dale brings you
THE TAGGARTS OF TEXAS!

Those Taggart men—strong, sexy and hard to resist...

You've met Jesse James Taggart in FIREWORKS!
Harlequin Romance #3205 (July 1992)

And Trey Smith—he's THE RED-BLOODED YANKEE!
Harlequin Temptation #413 (October 1992)

And the unforgettable Daniel Boone Taggart in SHOWDOWN!
Harlequin Romance #3242 (January 1993)

Now meet Boone Smith and the Taggarts who started it all—
in LEGEND!
Harlequin Historical #168 (April 1993)

Read all the Taggart romances!
Meet all the Taggart men!

Available wherever Harlequin Books are sold.